Welcome to Piney Falls

PINEY FALLS MYSTERIES

JOANN KEDER

Welcome to

Piney Falls

This story is a work of fiction. Names, characters, places and events described herein are the product of the author's imagination or are used fictitiously. Any resemblance to actual events, locations, organizations or persons is entirely coincidental.

Welcome to Piney Falls

Edited by: Sara Williams

Cover Design by Molly Burton with Cozy Cover Designs

Publisher: Purpleflower Press

ISBN: 978-1-7336639-4-6

The Case of the Vegan Vixen

The Case of the Cream Cheese Caper

<u>*Cont'd*</u>

<u>Pepperville Stories</u>

The Story of Keilah

Secrets and Sunflowers

Franniebell and Purple Wonder

The Something That Happened in Pepperville

Be the first to hear about new releases!

www.joannkeder.com

For Andy

Acknowledgments

Special thanks to my Advance Reader Team – the Keder Readers! Historical resources were graciously provided by Marcy Dunning at the Columbia River Maritime Museum and Liisa Penner from the Heritage Museum, both located in Astoria, Oregon. Other cherished humans who willingly share from their immense well of knowledge: Nichelle Paz, Jenny Smith, Barbara Carter, and my wonderful husband, Doug. As always, love and thanks to my family for all of their support. It takes more than one brain to produce a worthwhile story. There are certainly more people who were queried at least once and without hesitation, offered their expertise. Thank you all for your part in bringing this book to life!

"It is only through mystery and madness that the soul is revealed."
Thomas Moore

Dictionary

Bairn: baby or small child

sgian-dubh: A knife carried in the stocking by Highlanders

Fois shìorraidh gun robh aig a h-anam: her sould rest in peace

Strang: strong

Tantallion: A traditional Scottish cake

Bad bodie: A disparaging remark about a person

Chapter One

Shocking Discovery
Aisley Lumber Township Herald
November 13, 1925

Yesterday morning as Mrs. Edith Pressbone and her young son, Daltrey, were walking their dog next to our scenic falls, they happened upon a gruesome sight. There, before those tender eyes, were the remains of two women floating in the water. These were not mere vacationers to our lovely forest by the sea, but rather the matriarchs of our community.

After the administration of smelling salts by young Daltrey, Mrs. Pressbone found herself steady enough to make her way back to town and the comforting arms of her husband. He, along with local authorities were able *to identify the half-clothed corpses of Faye Scheddy, also known as Faye Flanagan, and her sister, one Fiona Scheddy, née Flanagan.*

Upon closer inspection, the ill-fated crew discovered a pile of neatly folded underskirts and two pairs of black, sturdy boots on the rock above the falls. It was determined that the lost souls took their own lives sometime the previous night. The constable removed himself to 811 Flanagan Lane, the home the widows shared with their combined five children. To his surprise, the entire residence was devoid of human life. The furniture was covered as if the family had planned an extended holiday.

Both women were last seen at the cannery last week, conversing with long-time employee Samuel Li about the upcoming employee clam chowder night. Authorities plan to contact neighboring communities to ascertain the location and well- being of the children.

Mmes. Scheddy and Scheddy were something of local legend, raising families and contributing to daily operations at Scheddy Salmon Cannery after the deaths of their husbands some eight years past. In addition, their influence can be seen in many local charitable organizations, including Flanagan Lane Hospital and Aisley Lumber Township City School. The sisters were Scottish immigrants, entering the country as young brides in 1908.

It has also been reported that sometime during the evening of November 12th, Scheddy Cannery inexplic-

ably burned to the ground. It is unknown at this time if the two tragic events are somehow related. There have been no missing persons reported in regards to this event.

Chapter Two

PINEY FALLS, OREGON

"Ma'am, I asked for your credit card."

She taps the counter with a gnarled knuckle. She is wearing a green, square nametag, the top half covered over with orange tape. The writing next to the tape reads, "Hi, I'm Mabel!" and underneath, "Ask me about our Scheddy Burger. Now with Cheese."

I make a mental note to give the Spruce Bark Motel a bad review. I travel all the time for my job and I don't possess any tolerance for businesses that don't provide quality customer service. My reviews are always to the point and highly regarded. *Quaint, little hilltop motel in an out-of-the-way village. Beware of the* snippy *woman at the front desk.*

"Sorry. Guess I'm a little taxed. I've been driving for four days, all the way from Chicago. I've never been to the Oregon Coast before." I push my $250 blonde-and-brown highlights behind my ear, conscious of the fact that something-other-than-blonde roots may be showing. I didn't make it to the salon before I hastily left Chicago. My mother would have been horrified I let myself be seen as anything less than perfect. "I pictured the ocean but not all of these evergreen trees. Your little town is quite picturesque!"

Removing my Slate Concept Elite card from my wallet, I hand it to her and wait for the usual gasp. Only the top ten percent of the business elite carry this card, and out of that miniscule percentile, only a small percentage of those are women. There is no recognition; instead, she stares behind me, at something vastly more important than the live human in front of her.

Staff didn't engage with the customers at all.

"How long will you be staying with us?" she asks, not even bothering to look me directly in my eyes as she runs my card. "Not that we have lots of visitors this time of year. Usually it's raining every day. You lucked out."

If I were able to give no stars, I would.

"I'm here on vacation. Tomorrow I'll head over to the house I rented. I decided to write a little story about your town. A nice diversion from real life." Silence. I shake my head and let out a loud sigh. She doesn't seem to understand this is the international sign for irritation.

"Mmmm." She licks her finger and rips the credit card receipt from the machine. "Just sign here. Got yer key. There's breakfast here in the lobby. Oatmeal.

Some days we even have brown sugar for the top, if my son remembers." Her voice is as dead as her eyes.

Scant breakfast offerings. No variety. Owner finds most things more interesting than the guests keeping her in business.

Sometimes I play this game when I travel: If these people lived elsewhere, what job would most suit them? She seems best qualified to watch a dryer spin. She doesn't have the personality for hospitality. Or eating crackers. I decide to turn around and see what's so important behind me that she can't take her eyes off it. It's a picture window, framing the rolling Pacific Ocean. Beautiful, but not as exciting as someone paying her actual money.

Can't explain why this place stays in business, other than cheap lodging. This is the way horror movies begin. If that's the case, this will be my last review.

"I'm meeting with the mayor in the morning to discuss the change of the town's name from Flanagan to Piney Falls. A Mr. Brittan, I believe? He was very enthusiastic when we spoke. He said something about historical records he thought I'd find interesting. He was happy someone was finally wanted to learn about..."

She turns and walks away from me abruptly, heading into a room behind the desk. I've had some peculiar travel experiences in my fifteen years as marketing manager for the multi-national company, Work Ahead Office Supplies - The Most Profitable

Office Supply Chain in the World, but this one will have to be on top of that list.

In all of my years as a marketing manager, I've never been treated this rudely. Forget the view and find yourself a nice cabin in the woods where you'll be stabbed to death by a psychotic killer. Much less stress.

"It would be great if you could just point me toward my room!" I call. No response. "I've been driving all day and I could really use a bath and a restaurant recommendation!" I've been told people in small towns are strange. That wasn't far off the mark. I bend down to pick up my luggage, my back complaining from the long ride and the less-than-optimal mattress availability the night before. I suppose asking someone to help assist me with carrying my suitcases is out of the question.

I hear muffled voices. There's definitely a man along with the unpleasant woman I've already met. She's speaking to him in sharp tones.

I've always enjoyed horror movies. If all goes according to the 1940's horror classic, "Don't Look Over the Edge," starring Tulip Sloan, they'll be sharpening their knives right now.

"This here's Ed Junior. He's my son." He nods by way of a response. His eyes are equally dead. Perfect horror movie material.

I fall into business mode and immediately set my things down and stick out my hand. "Lanie Anders. Pleasure to meet you." Despite the pain, I push my shoulders back. I'm trying to meet his gaze, but it seems like it is a futile effort.

He doesn't acknowledge me either. "Mom says you were asking about the mayor?"

I'm confused. "Not asking; just making conversation. Do you work for him? I've heard people in small towns sometimes do double duty. I have an appointment with him tomorrow. We're supposed to discuss the name change of the town. I'm writing a little story for —"

"You won't be seein' him."

"Excuse me?"

"You won't be seein' him. Mr. Brittan turned up a floater this morning."

"I don't understand what you mean by 'a floater.' Is this some kind of recreational thing? Is he hurt?"

Ed Junior snorts. "I'd say hurt. He jumped last night. He's passed on. It's a pretty common thing 'round here. Guess some people can't handle life or whatever. My cousin ended up a floater nearly four years ago now. Everything seemed fine, and then he took his hike and jumped. No note or anything. We was plannin' to fish the next day. Best fishin' season in ten years."

I'm in shock. Did I say something to upset him? I just asked if I could come and have a conversation. Write a silly story and get my life back on track. "Oh, no. I was hoping to ask him some questions." *I'm so looking forward to sharing EVERYTHING with you, Ms. Anders. Your call couldn't be timelier.*

The lady crosses her arms. "Well, he wouldn't've told you nothin' anyway. You're better off talking to others who weren't in —" Ed Junior elbows her in the side.

"There's a tourist center downtown. You might look at that tomorrow."

"You don't understand. I drove all this way…I'm here to see him. I have an appointment."

The room is starting to spin. I can't breathe.

"Ma'am? Ma'am?"

Chapter Three

AISLEY LUMBER TOWNSHIP, OREGON

Dearest Da,

What can a dochter say after a two-year silence?

It was so incredible, the circumstance that brought us across the sea, half a world from our life on the farm in our Scottish homeland. Mam always said her dochters would marry American men and return to her homeland. All the neighbors laughed, knowing who she was.

When two such men appeared in Brover's Pub, I thought it was some kind of magic Mam conjured up from the grave. The Scheddy boys - tall, thin, and serious Charles, and his brother Albert Todd, short and hearty in both laughter and belly, proposed taking your dochters to the new world barely a month later. You didn't even blink. You knew of Mam's dreams, always supporting her no matter the circumstance, and your only wish was for it to come true. Fois shìorraidh gun robh aig a h-anam, or as we say here, rest her soul in peace.

It made my heart tender when you sent us off with your most prized possession, the pearl-handled *sgian-dubh* Mam gave you for your wedding gift. Charles thought it best to keep such a fine knife nearby during our long journey since he realized it meant so much to you. Things held close to heart and mind are stolen in the blink of an eye in this busy city. The splendid silver ring Mam wore was a perfect gift for Charles and me. We shall treasure it always.

You told me to leave the farm and family in my bonnie Scotland to the back of my memory, and that's just what I did for a time. I couldn't bear the thought of forgetting you. It's been quite an adventure in this new land. I'm sorry, as simple as it sounds. Maybe hearing of our experiences will help you to understand my lack of correspondence.

You'll find my language quite changed. I've warked hard to learn the words and ways of the country. Charles even tells me he forgets for a time that I started my life in the Scottish Lowlands. Thank you for making sure Sister Faye and I went all the way through primary school in Dundee so we would be properly prepared for a life off the farm. It wasn't easy for you to spare the labor but you knew educated girls could make a future for themselves.

After you gave your blessing for us to leave the manas for the new world, we traveled by ship to New York. Soon after, Charles said we should make our union official, so the four of us went to the courthouse and had a quiet wedding. Sister Faye and Alfred Todd took the ferry round the harbor to celebrate. Charles and I walked through the neighborhood instead, supping by candle as we stared out the window at the people of all shapes and colors hurrying by. Everyone in this country has to be somewhere quickly it seems.

It is a noisy city, New York, with the smells of the entire country all within a city block. Stacks upon stacks of people living in buildings that could touch the clouds. There are beautiful languages flowing from their mouths like music. Our neighbors just above are newly arrived from Italy. They all wark in the shoe factory, the faither cutting and his three sons piecing them together. The poor wife carries one bairn on her hip, and the other pulls at her skirt all day as she warks in the laundry.

The brothers are lively and engaging, eager to embark on the next chapter in their adventures. So much so that Sister Faye and I are sometimes near exhaustion at the end of each day. That's how they swept us off our feet, promising we'd see things never imagined in our small lives. Every day we grow more accustomed to their ways.

We both found jobs mending clothes. It is a basket without a bottom, but guid enough money to put food in our bellies. It gives us something to do while we learn all we can about our surroundings.

The boys leave for weeks at a time, which Sister Faye and I find a respite from their constant joviality.

The last trip, they returned with wild stories of big bison in the west. They brought home a robe for us each, made from the sturdy hide of the animal. Albert Todd acted out his meeting with the mighty stud while Charles cowered in the corner, folding his long limbs up into his torso, trying to make us believe he left his brother to deal with the wild bison on his own. Sister Faye and I were happy to stay in home where the only wild animals were children escaping with glee from the upstairs apartment.

On one occasion, Charles came back with a flush to his cheeks. He'd heard about an untamed part of the country, as far away from New York as is possible in this land of possibility. There were more fish than could be imagined, just waiting for the hardy soul with a business mind to come and harvest them. The only way to reach this area was across the country, first by train, and then by wagon ride, to a small village perched between mountain and ocean.

They told us we would encounter ruffians unlike those we knew from the pubs round our home, but Sister Faye and I have never been scared away easily. I haven't, anyway. You taught us that, Da. Face things head on. Be the strang, proud women Mam raised us to be.

Sister Faye liked the city life and was a wee bit unsure of the wildness of a faraway place. Alfred Todd pulled the bison hide coat over his head, used his chubby fingers as horns and charged at Sister Faye. She screamed, terrified of what might come next. She's been a bit sairr ever since that day in the barn. We always knew how to handle it in our home. To her husband it was a sign she was weak.

"I didn't marry a weak woman. You're not afraid of things, Faye." He hugged her shoulders tight until she stopped trembling. "Now that you've survived a wild animal, wife, you're brave enough to travel west."

She looked at him with seriousness. I wondered if the lass needed to rest and think about things. Then, true to her nature, Sister Faye began laughing until her eyes ran with tears. Alfred Todd showed her a picture postcard. It was taken through thick trees, a small forest window framing the vast ocean.

We knew it was where we were meant to find our fortunes, to make a name for the American side of the Flanagan family. For the next week, we dreamed of the wealth awaiting us. Sister Faye and I, the dochters of a sheep farmer, seemed destined for wealth and wonder.

Though we spoke of our dreams, Sister Faye's not a good one for change, despite the fact she came across the ocean to her new home with a husband she'd only known for a month. What keeps her going is the resolve to honor Mam's wishes, to become a part of her homeland.

We rode the train across this beautiful country, so vast and full of rolling hills like home. After following the thick, green forest for nearly a day, we got off the train in Astoria, Oregon, our legs still trying to continue the rhythm of the tracks. We felt like we'd reached the end of the world.

The boys rented a wagon and horses to carry all of our trunks. Charles used his map to find our way south, down the Oregon Coast. The large cliffs were blanketed by tall trees, so thick it's hard to tell there is even ground underneath.

We took a narrow path, between the great sea and the carpet of trees. Roads are still being constructed and the lumber industry is only slowed by the need for more hard workers. The best part, Da, is that the government offers free land for strang young men willing to clear it of the mighty trees and build homes.

After a day traveling rough roads, we stopped to camp overnight away from the imposing waves. Charles insisted we sleep as far into the trees as possible, away from the sight of those looking to steal the possessions of innocent travelers.

We awoke to an unwelcome sight. The ground beneath the wagon was wet, the ocean reaching up to greet its' new family. Albert Todd said it was a guid lesson about learning when the tide comes in. The hems of our skirts, Sister Faye and I, were damp. The horses were up to their knees in sandy soil. After two hours of pulling at the mud with our bare hands, we were able to dig them out. We thanked the heavens nothing worse happened.

We continued our journey, marveling at the rugged terrain. The water snaked along the bumpy road, babbling brooks to our left and roaring ocean to our right. After another half-day's ride, taking care to remove ourselves from the ocean side during the high tide, we came over a hill to see evidence of human life once again. Tall chimneys, the sound of lumber being hewn and the voices of the men who cut it.

As we approached, a thick pine smell filled our nostrils. Hemlock trees, we were later told. They are a tall pine in the shape of a perfect pyramid, with purplish or reddish-brown bark and slender drooping branches.

Soon we heard boisterous voices and breathed in the strang scent of fresh-cut wood. It was a welcome sound to our travel-weary ears. A carved wooden sign greeted this weary group of travelers: Aisley Lumber Township.

Men were still furiously building a road into toon but we were able to make our way around the confusion. To my left were houses stretching up the hillside, each more colorful than the last. Plenty of majestic green trees in between each, mind you.

Besides the sounds, a magnificent view greeted our eyes. We were at an inlet where the ocean tucked further intae the land, causing the endless tall trees to force their way further intae the hills. To my right, the gentle bay, quiet blue for as far as the eye could see. After the barren miles of ocean seen during our trip to America, these changes in landscape were welcome. And Da, just as it was in New York, the toon was full of people from all different countries.

We forgot our exhaustion as we marveled at the bustling scene. There we found a large lumber mill. The tall, white chimney, billowing steam was our first sight. I asked Charles if we might watch as they did their wark. Since he was just as tired as I, he thought that a grand idea before we found a place to sup for the night.

A man on a small boat pushed logs a quarter acre long from a small stream into the tall building. As the steam hissed, pulleys removed the log from the water and onto a set of tracks not unlike the ones we left just a day earlier.

Swirling circular blades came down from the ceiling tightening, as they got closer. The log was pushed in and then out of this mass of cutlery until all the bark from the tree was removed. A man of considerable size oversaw the entire operation. He looked back, surprised to see two women so interested in his job, but nodded in approval.

As we got closer, we could see them planing the wood, cutting down large half-pieces of trees to make them smaller and smoother until they reached the desired size. Sister Faye and I were fascinated by this big piece of machinery, so powerful and the men who fed the strang-smelling pines through them. After several rounds of shaving and sanding, the finished long squares were transported on rollers down to the dock where more strang men waited to load them onto the cart to be placed on a ship.

Albert Todd, impatient to experience more of our new city, waited at the dock for us to finish. When the three of us walked away from the mill, we barely had our senses. The buzzing, whooshing and clanking of the factory along with the men trying to yell over the noise was too much for ears still recovering from the constant loud sound of the train hurtling down the tracks.

We noticed Albert Todd talking to a small, finely dressed man. When the man turned to greet us, I stifled a giggle. He looked just like a mouse, with a pinched-up face, a pointed nose, and small, beady eyes. His thick, bushy mustache twitched when he spoke.

I could barely make out his conversation, with the noises of the lumber mill and my overworked ears. Words were exchanged and then the men looked at me. I smiled helplessly. Thank guidness for Charles' booming voice. "This is Mr. Stanford Aisley. He owns the mill. He's invited us to stay with them for the night."

I was so embarrassed. I shook his hand - a soft, moist hand that seemed fitting for a mouse of a man. "Charmed to meet you, Mrs. Scheddy. We'll be most honored to host you this evening." He didn't smile at me, but his mustache quivered.

My shoulders twitched at just that moment. You used to chide me for those feelings. Mam and I both got them, you remember? They only occur when someone bad got a little too close.

Your Devoted Dochter,
Fiona Flanagan Scheddy

Chapter Four

CHICAGO

Two Months Earlier

I clear my throat. "I'll start, I guess. I'm imagining this story could be about a town with a mystery. Maybe a murder. They changed their name from...." I scan the document, denying the need for the red-plastic glasses sitting in my purse. I hope I get the letters in the correct order. "Hmmm...Flanks to Piney Falls. Well, that will be easy. It will be a murder. Something really juicy."

Our middle-aged teacher announced the assignment earlier in the evening to a lukewarm reception. He handed a large, black cap to the first person in my row. "I'm not doing magic tricks today. We're simply passing the hat so you may pick out an article. As creative writers, we're going to take these truths and make them fiction." He winked at me for the fourth or fifth time tonight, like he and I are co-parenting this night class. I'm here to learn, just like everyone else. I can't help it if they're all at least a decade younger than me.

"That's Flanagan, Lanie," the just-out-of-his teens guy who doesn't believe in deodorant corrects me.

I stare hard at the page. I refuse to bring out my readers in front of this impossibly youthful-looking group. They may see it as a sign of weakness and pounce, like lions attacking an injured gazelle. "Oh, yes, you're right. It's Flanagan. I'll have to research this. Looks like a scenic place on the Oregon Coast. What does everyone else think about my mystery idea? Maybe a murderer in their midst? A real whodunnit?"

The lady with six kids who are constantly texting her nods.

I look pointedly at the "No phones in class please!" sign above her head.

"You bet. Sounds like a good plan," she says, staring at her screen.

"No, that doesn't make any sense." Stinky Guy leans against the brick wall and folds his arms across his puny chest. "Murders happen all the time in every city. You've gotta come up with something better than that, unless you're going to reboot that stupid old TV show my grandma used to watch. Towns don't just undergo a massive rebranding and take on a new identity every time there's a murder. Make it aliens versus humans. Give your story meaning."

"I think it's a great idea. I'd love to see what happens, Lanie!" Dancinee, the cute, twenty-something who always giggles when she has to speak in front of the class chimes in. I could use a cheerleader like her in the office. My last three assistants lost their jobs when they lost their inner perky.

"Well, what about everyone else? Ideas?" I'm used to taking charge as a marketing manager at Work Ahead Office Supplies - The Most Profitable Office Supply Chain in the World. I don't think twice about leading my group. We sit in awkward silence. As far as I understand, I'm the only one of them not taking this class to gain college credit. They seem to have forgotten this very important point. "C'mon, you guys can come up with something."

Stinky Guy puts his hands behind his head. Not a good move for someone with his hygiene issues. "I was considering writing mine about space wars. There's this galaxy where people only use ten words, but their body language when they talk is different for each meaning."

I glance at his article. The title is, *Young Girl Miraculously Survives Bridge Collapse.*

"Hey, I just had a thought." I push my hair behind my ears. "I'm spending the weekend downtown at the Plush Regency while they are remodeling the main floor of my house. What if you joined me for drinks tomorrow night and we could hash out our stories?"

"I think that's a great idea!" A voice that I dread booms from behind me. "I'd love to join you all, if that's okay. See what you come up with in a different setting."

Phone Lady sets her phone on the table. "You're buying?"

"Um... certainly. That's fine. We could meet for drinks in the bar around seven? I'll order appetizers. My treat as well."

Everyone nods.

On Saturday, after a full day of self-care that included having a massage, manicure, pedicure, and facial, I find myself actually looking forward to our meeting. I don't socialize, at least beyond what is required of me at work. It's too much after a full day of networking. That's how I know I'm good at my job. Great, in fact. I put everything I have into my work life.

I find the biggest table in the bar area and instruct the staff to place a large tray of vegetables and dip beside me. "Manhattan, please?" I say, remembering the last time I met colleagues for an after-conference drink and left with Red —or was it Fred —after four drinks. Not tonight.

The young man at the bar glances at me every now and then. Childhood flashbacks are inevitable. "You look just like that old-timey actress, if she had been chubby." I look down and pick absently at freshly-manicured nails. It's the same message I've heard my whole life, except that my mother would stand me in front of a mirror while telling me.

Luckily I packed dress casual for my weekend away. A beige, silk Shanel top and black skirt with black

Sinthia Propensia boots. My assistant waited in line four hours for these boots last Friday evening. Maybe I feel a twinge of guilt over my abuse of power. Lots of things have been circling my brain.

I've been thinking about Stinky Guy's comments. He's right. Towns don't just change their names. Not for a single murder. Why am I taking this so seriously? I could write about space aliens after four Manhattans. This is just a diversion from the stress of life. Remodeling stress. I glance at my black, vintage 1940 Dolex watch. 7:15. I feel a hand on my back.

"Hi Lanie. I can't stay long, but I didn't want you to worry that I'd forgotten." Dancinee - hair pulled up high in a tight bun and dramatic, purple eye shadow on her bright, brown eyelids - sits down beside me. Her caramel skin is glistening with something glittery. She is wearing a nametag that says, *"Hi, my name is Daphne! Ask me about our deals!"*

It's hard to hide my disappointment. "Oh, I guess you're the only one coming. I thought this would be fun."

She looks down at her brightly painted, orange fingernails. "Well, to be honest, it was a little...much. We're all college students. Just trying to get through class and work and kids. Nobody has extra time for stuff like this."

"Oh." I feel stupid. Of course, they're all busy. I'm at a different place in my life. Lots of money, and lots of spare time. "Well, can you at least sit for a minute and have a drink with me?"

"I can only stay for a couple of minutes. I've got to get to the casino. I work the late shift on Saturday nights. Best tips come after everyone is tanked." She smiles and I notice dimples on either side of her face. "You remind me so much of my grandma's favorite actress. She was in those black and white movies..."

"Tulip Sloan. 1940s icon who made thirty movies in five years. I get that a lot. My mother made me pose as Tulip and sign autographs in the mall every Saturday. *Sit up straight and suck your stomach in, Lanie. Your delivery has to be perfect.* I touch my round face self-consciously.

"Look, I didn't mean to make you feel bad. It was so nice of you to offer. But this is only a stupid easy assignment. I'll probably write it the night before class."

"What's your goal, Dancinee? After you're done with school?"

She looks taken aback. "Wow. Um...people don't usually ask that question in night school." She rubs the back of her neck and stares at the ground. "Well, I want to run a women's shelter. My mom was in an abusive relationship for six years. If she would have had someplace to go, you know? A safe place with the resources to help her keep her job and rebuild her life? She wouldn't have needed that jerk in her life. She would still have her original front teeth he knocked those out one night when he was drunk."

"Oh, sweetie, I'm so sorry." I reach over and touch her hand, squeezing it. That's something I learned in the seminar, *Connecting with the Hard-to-Reach Client.* I slept with Ron, the seminar organizer, that night. We practiced his patented hand-patting technique on all non-hand regions.

She uses her other hand to wipe the tears from her face. "No, it's okay. She's fine now. We're both okay. We're doing better. I just want to help other women, you know?"

"Can I ask, why does your nametag say, 'Daphne'? Do you have another name?"

She rolls her eyes. "That was my boss's idea. Makes me seem less ethnic."

"Did I miss the party?"

We turn our heads to see Carl Jackson, our Creative Writing professor. He is wearing a brown suit jacket and a teal shirt. It makes his alabaster skin appear slightly more human than the fluorescent lights of the college classroom. His thinning hair is parted on the side and covered in some kind of strongly scented gel. Dancinee stands and pushes her chair in. "Sorry, I've got to leave." Her cheery demeanor returns as she pulls her purse over her shoulder and turns to leave. "You guys have a great time! Nice to see you, Professor!"

He sits down beside me. His cologne, while competing for scent space with his hair gel, is a surprisingly intoxicating musky scent. "It looks like you didn't have much of a turnout. That's to be expected. Most people don't have the time, or frankly the interest, to invest in projects."

I'm at once irritated by his presence and happy that I'm not alone to stew in my pathetic-ness.

"Beer please," he calls to the bartender. "Whatever's on tap is fine."

"I'll take another Manhattan too."

"So, Ms. Anders. You seem a bit more, shall I say, 'seasoned' than most of the students I observe at the community college. I'm wondering what brought you to my Creative Writing 101 class?"

My mouth drops open. "Are you making a comment on my age? I'm certain we're in the same decade of life. And I really don't..."

He puts a hand up. "No, that's not what I meant. You're obviously a successful woman. Already well-trenched in a career is more what I meant."

For the second time tonight, I'm feeling like a fool. Not a position I occupy with ease. "Yes, you're right. I run the marketing department for Work Ahead Office Supplies - The Most Profitable Office Supply Chain in the World. I'm usually traveling, so the only hobby I have is redecorating my home. It's the big Victorian place up on the hill off Highway 78? I figure everyone knows that house. It's a conversation piece."

He nods.

"I decided I should expand my horizons beyond flying to Paris to look at tile samples." I take a drink of my second Manhattan, feeling vastly superior to this tiny, insignificant man.

He leans forward and puts his chin in his hand. "I've admired that home for years. A pretty iconic location, hosting the abolitionist meetings during the Civil War. You must be a history buff. You'll really have fun with the article you chose."

"The history of a little town in Oregon? I suppose it's a fun distraction." I finish my Manhattan and signal for one more. "Do you know anything about it? I did some preliminary research on the internet and didn't come up with anything."

He smiles and taps his finger on the table. "You must've forgotten the assignment. No further research. Take the article as is and craft your own story around it."

I straighten my top, feeling a little fuzzy. Hotel booze isn't usually so strong. I realize I haven't eaten anything since breakfast. When I'm not on the road, I have a very ordered existence and this hotel-at-home living has thrown me off my routine.

"I don't operate that way. I research everything. Schedule my day down to the minute. That's how I've gotten to the pinnacle of the marketing world. It must work because I don't fail. No surprises, no failure." His smile is starting to seem less irritating to me and perhaps slightly attractive.

"Okay, okay. You win. Why don't I help you? What if there were a really unusual reason for the change of name?"

"So, you do know something?" I try to sit up straight, and then realize things are starting to spin.

"Just a bit. I spent some time in Oregon when I was in college. As a summer project, several of my buddies went to the coast to help rebuild a community center that was hit by a terrible windstorm. On our day off we drove up the hill to the former home of one of the town's founders. It used to be Flanagan Lane Hospital. The main building itself was still standing, but everything around it was mostly a pile of kindling after this big storm. Such a pity. The townsfolk said the place was cursed. They wouldn't get into specifics. And the falls..."

His words are starting to swirl around my head in a way that feel like a gigantic European traffic circle. "I'm so sorry, Mr. Jackson. I'm not feeling at all well. I'm wondering if you would mind accompanying me to my room?"

I can't see the expression on his face, but I know he has paused for a considerable amount of time. I also realize I need to lie down soon or I won't be able to make it all the way to the seventh floor.

"I should've warned you before that last Manhattan. The bartender over there is Chandler Norris. Took my Modern Writing course last semester and wrote every paper about finding the cheapest beer in the city. I'm sure his bartending skills aren't up to par."

"If you can't take me, I'm sure the staff wouldn't mind..." I grasp my head to stop it from spinning, but it doesn't seem to be working.

"No, I'm more than happy to escort you." He comes over to my side of the table and puts my arm around his shoulder, grateful he is slightly shorter and I can lean on him. He places my black Sandra Mason

Limited Edition bag on his other arm; I can only think about what would happen if one of my colleagues happens to be in the bar, watching this spectacle. Thankfully, there's not enough of me present to experience shame.

As we make our way to the elevator, and finally to my room, he helps me put the key in the door and then tries to stand still while I make my way in. "Come on in," I motion.

"I don't want to be inappropriate. You're not exactly..."

"Get in here," I command. I've never been turned down, sober or drunk.

He doesn't take much persuading. I've had more experience than he has, that's evident even in my state of inebriation. When we are done, I roll away from him, hoping for a blissful sleep that will result in a single dent in the mattress.

The next morning, I awake to pounding on my door. I look at the clock. Ten-thirty. I forgot to put the Do Not Disturb sign on the door. "What??" I yell.

The knocking continues, despite my protests. It is relentless. Maybe I ordered room service and forgot. I turn over and notice an empty side of the bed. There is a note, "Thank you for last night. You were right; it was best I leave."

I always have a twinge of guilt the next morning, but it quickly disappears after my second cup of coffee. I pride myself on the ability to walk away, no matter the level of attraction. I don't want the unknowns that a relationship would require. Looking for someone else to tell me what I already know. No thanks.

I pull on my robe and smooth down my unruly, wavy hair, just yesterday perfectly styled for our meeting. I pause for a moment in front of the long mirror facing the bathroom. I'm not bad for a hungover forty-year-old. My peach skin is still glowing from the facial. My cute, upturned nose the plastic surgeon called his masterpiece, (You're sure I still look like Tulip Sloan? Identical, Lanie. If she weren't so thin.) is covered with mascara. My green eyes are a little worse for the wear, but I have special drops to fix that. I'm reluctant to open the door without my full makeup compliment, thanks to eighteen years of scrutiny by a mother expecting perfection. I apply a quick swipe of Ruby Mist lipstick and pull open the door.

It's a man in uniform. "Miss Anders? We've been trying to reach you all night. Your home caught fire. I regret to inform you, there's nothing left."

Chapter Five

AISLEY LUMBER TOWNSHIP, OREGON

Dearest Da,

After our tour of Aisley Lumber Mill, our adventure in Aisley Lumber Township had just begun. We followed Mr. Stanford Aisley, the logging company owner, down the next street and up a winding road. An ornately carved wooden sign announced, "Aisley Drive" as we climbed higher up the hill. To have a street named after you in this big country is quite an accomplishment. Especially for a little mouse like Mr. Stanford Aisley.

Oh, Da. It was such a grand home. Painted buttercup yellow and three stories. It has a turret on the side and a quaint, round porch surrounding the cylindrical portion of the house. There are tall windows everywhere, to view the ocean, I guessed.

The door opened and a miniature creature tiptoed out to greet us. A milk-faced delicate woman with miniature brown curls framing her face, she looked like she was made in a factory to match Mr. Stanford Aisley. She grasped our palms, Sister Faye and I, with her dainty ones. I feared our sturdy farm hands might crush hers. Terrible to admit, but I searched under her petite nose for mouse whiskers. Later I told Sister Faye, and she admitted she did the very same thing.

Mrs. Aisley's voice was tiny, just like her body. Her mouth barely opened to let words slip out. After our loud day, I could barely make out her words.

"So happy to meet you dears. I'm Violet Aisley. You'll find yourself most welcome in our home."

Mr. Stanford Aisley explained his wife agreed to marry and leave her father's mansion after he promised to build her a home equal in stature overlooking the ocean. She blushed slightly and nodded.

I was ashamed of the sight of us–grimy from our long adventure across this wondrous land and just the night before sleeping in the woods. She didn't say a thing, being a woman of high society, as she showed us to the second floor, where two bedrooms, each with its own lavvy, were prepared for our arrival.

Mr. Stanford Aisley wouldn't have had time to send word we were coming, but things were prepared for us as if he had. Even more impressive, there were two stylish, green frocks laid out—one on each bed. I didn't ask why, but was indebted to this woman we'd just met.

After lavender-scented baths in fine porcelain tubs, we went down for dinner in the large, formal dining room. Mr. and Mrs. Aisley spoke in small-rodent whispers, in contrast to the booming voices of our husbands and the loud laughter Sister Faye and I shared.

"Such nicely fashioned logs," Charles remarked, looking around the ornately decorated room. He slapped his brother on the back. I winced. Even a farm lass named Fiona knows when to keep thoughts to herself.

"Not much tree left in them." Albert Todd replied, causing Sister Faye to guffaw. I chuckled into my napkin. Mr. Stanford Aisley looked at us in disapproval when we laughed at our husbands' remarks. Mrs. Aisley wiped her mooth nervously.

"How'd ye meit each other?" I asked to break the tension.

"My father owned Van Brasen Lumber Mill in Seattle. The largest lumber company in the west," Mrs. Aisley said somewhat boldly. "Mr. Aisley came to conduct private business with him. I was there to bring him notice of a formal dinner that night. Father thought it wise for Mr. Aisley to attend. He encouraged our marriage, to merge the two lumber dynasties intae one family." She looked over at Mr. Stanford Aisley, who nodded.

I thought our arrangement to be out-of-the-ordinary, but theirs was nothing more than a business transaction.

"A man has little if he doesn't have a name," Mr. Stanford Aisley remarked out of nowhere.

"We take pride in the Scheddy name," Alfred Todd

replied, his mooth full of half-cooked beef.

"The toon has my name on it until the end of time. When I married Violet, her father wanted the town to become Van Brasen, after his family. No sir, I told him. No bride is worth a man's name." He glared at his wife. "He realized he would never find a better husband for an old maid of twenty."

Mrs. Aisley's pale cheeks turned red, but she said nothing. Poor lass. To spend her days with such an awful man didn't seem worth having a 'Mrs.' in front of her name.

We finished our meal in silence, being too tired to keep up with the light banter. After a tense dessert, I offered to help Mrs. Aisley clean up. "Oh no, dears, that's for the maids." Can you imagine, Da?

The next morning, Charles and Albert Todd wanted us to view the location where our cannery would be. We walked down a steep incline until we reached the flat ground, hearing the whir of the lumber mill once more. Albert Todd motioned us to walk further, down the dirt street and past several *hoose ay nae weel reputen*, here called 'brothels.' Sister Faye turned her head away. I was fascinated by the women posed on balconies overlooking the street. Some of them were quite beautiful, though I could see the sadness in their eyes as they watched us walk freely through toon, grasping the hands of our beloved men.

Albert Todd pointed out a newly-built dock. There was a bare piece of ground next to it, where we would build our business. There were already men working on our building, OUR cannery. The boys said they would meet up with us later and encouraged us to go exploring.

Before we left, Mrs. Aisley arranged for her maid to make us a basket of dried salmon, blueberries and freshly baked sourdough bread. "There are waterfalls back in these hills, dearies. The natives think they have powers to heal." She pointed upward, what seemed like an impossibly steep climb we hadn't taken in our months walking flat city blocks.

"The first you'll see is Little Cone. It's the easiest walk. Then, nigh a mile further, you'll find the tall wonder. It lands on rocks built by the ancient gods before splashing further to the ground. Wondrous. That one is called Piney Falls."

Sister Faye and I, having spent our days nested behind sewing machines, were eager for such a challenge. First, we walked to Little Cone Falls. It is called a cascade, a series of small falls. There is a short drop, then another hop to a fall of the same size. These steps continue four times. It is surrounded by such lush foliage we felt as though we had come upon the Garden of Eden itself.

We continued on, stopping several times to catch our breath and push aside the tall green grasses that descend over the worn pathway. When we reached the top, Piney Falls was indeed a view to behold. The sound of the rushing water was at first overwhelming to the city ear. After we stood for a few minutes, a calm overtook us. The water flows violently down the side of the cliff, splashing on imposing rocks midway before careening to the wide pool of water below. It is a sight neither Sister Faye nor I could imagine to be real. Violent, exciting, calming, and intoxicating.

The thought of a new life in this magical place overwhelmed me. The salt of my tears touched my lips before Sister Faye wiped them with her skirt. I didn't want to leave, but I knew we must.

As we began to make our way back down the steep hill, we encountered a pleasant man with tan skin and happy eyes collecting mushrooms. He suggested we take another way to the bottom. "Easier walk. Find your picture," he said, nodding. Sister Faye and I looked at each other, not understanding what he might be inferring. I asked where he might be from. Though we traveled from one coast to the other, I hadn't heard this accent before.

"China," he replied, answering my unvoiced question. I'd only read of that country in our geography studies at school. I'd never actually seen anyone from there.

"You speak our language, in your land?" Sister Faye was just as excited as I.

He shook his head. "English words for English world. I speak Chinese in homeland." Sister Faye continued to quiz him until I could tell he was uncomfortable. He told us his name was Samuel "American name I chose" Li, and he worked for a cannery but they didn't pay well. He was excited to learn we would be opening Scheddy Salmon Cannery soon. Faye promised him we would pay a fair wage, even though we had no idea what that might be. Mr. Samuel Li assured us we would meet him again.

Sister Faye and I took his advice and headed down the other trail at a much more enjoyable slope. We stopped before we reached the bottom, about halfway, on a large, flat piece of ground. I hadn't shared with Charles or Faye, but when we arrived to such steep terrain, I began to wonder about finding a piece of land to claim as our own.

We walked in silence, each enjoying the scenery. Sister Faye pulled on my sleeve. "Our photograph!" She pointed through a hole in the trees, seemingly created for us. We could see the ocean in all of its glory. It looked just the same as the picture postcard the boys gave us. Around us was flat land, enough for two homes and space to grow whatever we might need to eat after we cleared the trees. We looked at each other, thinking the same thing.

We brought our husbands up the next day for a picnic. We both carefully prepared them to receive our opinions while deciding such opinions were their very own.

We picnicked, all four happy as the clams nestled under the sand on the beach. Sister Faye and I are so lucky to have such hard-working husbands, not afraid to go out in the world and make their mark. It feels as though nothing will stop the Flanagan sisters.

Your Devoted Dochter,

Fiona Flanagan Scheddy

Chapter Six

AISLING LUMBER TOWNSHIP

Aisling Lumber Township Herald
November 20th, 1925

Readers have had a week to comprehend the deaths of our dear matriarchs, Fiona and Faye Flanagan, as they wished to be known. We have uncovered more about the fate of their offspring, five between them. Sarah, Walter, Shaw, children of Fiona and her husband, Charles, and Percival and Padrug, sons of Faye and Albert Todd, are found to be residing in Portland at 1112 Poplar Tree Drive.

Sarah, the oldest sibling and cousin, confessed her mother and aunt instructed the children to remove themselves to the city of Portland to continue their educations. The children were given a large stipend and told to take their treasured possessions to their new establishment, as the matriarchs would soon be joining them.

The children were shocked when told the fate of their mothers. They learned Faye and Fiona had paid each

38

child's full tuition at Chatwell School for the duration of their educations. All will be well-cared for. The Scheddy offspring do not wish to return to Aisley Lumber Township for the time being. They asked the town make donations to City School and Flanagan Lane Hospital in the names of their dearly departed mothers. As all can imagine, the children are devastated beyond words.

A private service will be held in Portland with only the children in attendance.

Chapter Seven

PINEY FALLS, OREGON

Present Day

I've made a list of all local restaurants and other things you may find helpful during your time in Piney Falls. Please enjoy your stay! Smiley face. Smiley face. *Sincerely, Proud Homeowner.*

I sit down on the massive mattress in this exquisitely decorated modern-style home and marvel at its design. The bed is more comfortable than my $9,000 Comfortesque Deluxe. I make a mental note to get the name of the model to buy for my new home.

My home. My insides twist and turn every time I think about it. I've had strange dreams ever since it happened, probably because I refuse to let my mind go there during my waking hours. Did I cause my house to burn down? Because I was so entrenched in my business life, my routine, that I wasn't paying attention?

I passed out in the motel lobby last night. First time in my entire life I lost consciousness like that. I woke to the smell of Ed Junior waving some kind of substance—illegal I'm sure—under my nostrils. His arm hair, impossibly long, tickled my cheek. If they would have just given me my key and directions to a restaurant, I would have been fine. I don't like feeling out of control like that.

Ma'am, can we call the ambulance for you? It's a brand-new vehicle. Our hospital is top notch.

Grudgingly, I head back to my car to retrieve my bags. I bought three suitcases, each labeled according to importance. Suitcase One: every toiletry I might need in this remote little hamlet, because petroleum jelly is no substitute for eye cream. Suitcase Two: An outfit for every type of occasion; formal, casual, and daily wear. Suitcase Three: coordinating shoes for Suitcase Two. I hope it's enough. I've never actually stayed somewhere without a valet.

I feel rugged and independent unloading my own luggage into the driveway. There is a sudden, sharp pain in my back. I haven't had my bi-weekly massage since before the fire. Last night's drama flashes through my head one more time. I bend down slowly to pick them up. "Oh, crap." I wince.

I sense strange hands on my spine. They put pressure in just the right spot, easing the pain immediately. "Breathe deep with me. Hooooo. Ooooh."

I take a couple of deep breaths into my lungs and find, to my surprise, it does help. "Oh, thank you so much. Too many days in the car I suppose. I'm Lanie. If you're not a professional massage therapist, you missed your calling."

I turn around to see a fluorescent-green jumpsuit, improbably attached to a woman with uncontrolled hair and big-framed green, plastic glasses.

"November Bean. Most just call me Vem. She sticks a thin hand in mine, sweaty from working her magic on my back. She is solid, without one ounce of fat on her diminutive body. "I've taken a lot of classes in massage, but no, I've never done it professionally." I can't stop staring at her. In the city, women would pay thousands of dollars to a trainer and nutritionist to look that way. The only wide part of her body is her incredibly thick and out-of-control hair.

"What an unusual name. Do your siblings have unusual names too?"

She looks away. "Why don't I help you with your bags? I've got an hour before my yoga class. I'm your next-door-neighbor, by the way. Not to be weird, but I can see in your living room window. You're quite the stunner. Reminds me of old Hollywood, what with your rosebud lips and high cheekbones."

I wait for the inevitable comment about my non-Hollywood-shaped body. It doesn't come.

"I don't mind nudity. I celebrate the body," she continues. "Just letting you know; in case a free show isn't your thing." She lets out a loud honk, an assault to this otherwise peaceful spot. I jump back, startled but she doesn't seem fazed.

"I'll keep that in mind when I decide to go 'natural.' I sure had a hard time finding this place."

I motion to my trunk and Vem pulls the final, gigantic bag out, not letting it touch the ground. "Anything else?" she asks. I shake my head. She pushes one suitcase under her arm and wheels the other two up the hill.

"No surprise you had trouble finding the place. Magnificent Drive used to be Flanagan Lane. The powers that be wanted to give the whole town a makeover, I guess." We walk up the hill toward my front door, which sits on the only flat piece of ground within my view.

"That's why I'm here, actually. I'm taking a little break from life. I'm going to write a story about your town. Why it changed its name." I'm out of breath and need to stop before we reach the ten steps up to the door. "Wait, please." I gasp. Walking the slight incline of city streets in heels, no matter how many blocks, has not prepared me for this terrain.

She stops and puts the suitcase on the ground. "Why would you want to do that?"

I'm embarrassed that I have to catch my breath. When I stand again, I see her face is serious. "It's just a fun project. Things have been a little challenging for me lately. I needed a diversion."

"Oh. Well, you won't find much. There was a big fire that destroyed a lot of the town's historical records. I just moved back myself. Grew up here and moved to California with my parents shortly after my seventeenth birthday. Didn't look back once I left. Sometimes Piney Falls is best viewed from the rear-view mirror."

I pick up my purse and continue toward the door, but she seems planted in one spot and doesn't let me move around her.

"What brought you back to this area, Vem?"

She shrugs nonchalantly. "Divorce. Needed to hit the reset button."

I maneuver around her and open the door. The house is set in the side of the hill, with one large main floor and a downstairs area with two bedrooms. It's spacious and lovely. When I open the dusty blue curtains, there is a breathtaking view of the ocean. I suck in the air too fast and end up coughing until Vem comes and puts fingers on either side of my throat. "Take in a few deep breaths," she commands. In a few moments, the coughing is gone. "You never get tired of that view." She says wistfully. "Washes over the bad memories. At least for a time."

"Thank you, Vem." I think about what has transpired the last twenty-four hours. "The mayor ... did you know him?"

"Mmmhmmm." Her eyes glaze over, like she's a million miles away.

"Why would he just end things like that?" Silence. "Vem?"

"Oh, there have been lots of suicides around town. It's such a common thing here that nobody thinks twice about it anymore."

"Like a curse?" I blush, remembering my night with my creative writing teacher. "Why would you want to come back then? That sounds awfully depressing."

"It's not this place. Well, not Piney Falls the town. It's the legend of The Flanagan sisters. They were so depressed by the deaths of their husbands and the cannery fire that they decided they couldn't go on. People use that as an excuse to do crazy things. You know how it is."

I can't understand why the whole town would be okay with that. "It seems strange to me. The mayor dies and nobody bats an eye."

"You haven't been in Piney Falls very long. It will make sense when you reach the end. Although, the end is just an illusion. Did you know that?"

"Right." I look at something vague behind her, not wanting to engage in this discussion.

"I'm glad you're here, Lanie. I was feeling a little down today. It's good to have a friend."

I'm surprised she's made the leap to friendship and my bags aren't even unpacked yet. "Yes...I'm sure we'll be friends." I reply absently. "I'm going to do some research tomorrow. I might need your help."

I remember Dancinee at the end of a long day, needing someone to listen. I stop and turn around. "What's got you down?" I ask, not really interested in the answer.

She begins backing out of the house and pauses for a moment. "Nope. The moment is gone." She is on the top step now. I'm a little worried she'll fall. "We'll have deep discussions later on. I can see you are a true diamond underneath all of that fluff. Come over any time!" She backs quickly down the rest of the steps and waves as she runs toward her house.

I get into my car, happy it is a short drive down the hill and around a bend to the main street in town. Main, or Pine, Street is lined with colorful, clapboard storefronts. Quaint, like some of the little villages in Europe I've visited while on a quest for the perfect accouterments for my living room. There are several stores that don't look large enough to house any kind of retail location, but inside are two-person tables and shelves filled with local crafts. Every other storefront displays a "Welcome" flag fashioned of blue fabric. The alternating businesses have a "To Piney Falls" flag in green. It's all so charming. Why aren't the streets lined with tourists?

I walk down all seven blocks and then back up the other side of the street, pausing in front of a quaint park, smaller than the lot size of my home. A plaque rests on a cement pillar sitting at the entrance. It is covered by a wooden board, with the words, "City of Piney Falls, Piney Park" spray-painted over the top. Someone has pried a corner of the board loose, so I pull it up just enough to read the words underneath.

Piney Park is located on the grounds of the former Flanagan City School. This was the first school in the area to accept children of all nationalities.

I hear a car door shut behind me, but I want to read the date of the plaque, so I pull the board up slightly higher, causing it to crack.

"Ma'am, you need to back away slowly and put your hands up."

Chapter Eight

PINEY FALLS, OREGON,

Present Day

The next morning, I walk slowly to Vem's house, another uphill jaunt. I'm still trying to process what happened yesterday.

"Ma'am, I'll have to take you in for destruction of public property."

"But I didn't do anything. It was already damaged. I would think you would know that, Officer."

He shrugs his skinny shoulders. I can see he is wearing a nametag next to his badge. "Welcome to Piney Falls! I'm Paul! Ask me about our haunted tours."

"Look, Officer, there's no need for a weapon. I'm just a tourist, out exploring your quaint little town. I'll gladly pay for a new board. If you'll please..."

"Tourist? Why didn't ya say so?" He puts his weapon back in its holster. "Thought you might be related to those cult members. They seem to be multiplyin' by the

day - a cousin here, a nephew there. Can't rid ourselves of them." He pulls a wrinkled paper from his pocket. "Gotta read this," he whispers. "It's a city ordinance." He clears his throat and begins:

"Piney Falls was founded twenty years ago. Named after the scenic falls at the top of the hill," he points over his shoulder. "Our community was formerly known for its logging. Today, you can enjoy hiking, biking, and fishing. John Bowers, over there," he points again, this time vaguely over my left shoulder, "can arrange for any tours you want to take. Don't miss Cosmic Cakes and Antiquery. Best pastries on the coast." He puts the paper in his breast pocket and tips his hat.

"But what about Flanagan? Wasn't that the name of your city for almost one hundred years? It says so on this plaque you've worked so hard to cover."

He turns his head away from me and puts his hands on his hips. "Please enjoy your stay. And that'll be forty-five dollars for destruction of public property. You can pay that at the tourism center just down the street."

I have to fight my way through Vem's front yard, a place where yard ornaments have gone to die. Things are whirling and chirping, and I'm afraid of stepping on something that might be a prized toy.

When I ring the doorbell, it's the tune to a cereal commercial from my childhood, *Fruity Boats float into your tummy, tastin' so yummy, makes the best of your morn, made from real corn.* Good memories filter in: sitting on my father's lap while he read the morning paper, slurping my sugared cereal. He stroked my hair and told me I would be someone important someday.

Vem throws the door open wide, startling me with her appearance. She is wearing a turquoise turban and matching leggings. She has two coconut shells covering her breasts, but nothing else. Her glasses are square, aqua-colored plastic.

I can turn a giggle into a cough like the best executive after a six-martini lunch. "Good morning, Vem. I was wondering if you might give me some directions. I need to get to the history center. I looked it up and there's…"

"No good directions. It's the Piney Falls way of doing things. Get used to that. Nobody wants you to know how to get where you're going here. The longer you're lost, the more ways you'll find to spend your money." She adjusts her coconuts. "I'm just getting ready for my Happy Morning to You meditation in the back yard. Have to wear what makes me feel closest to Mother Earth."

I nod. "I get it." I don't. "Do you know where I need to go?"

"Yeah, just down the hill, take a left, head into town and take the first left and a quick right. It's a big white building that says, Re-integration Center. You can't miss it."

"What does that mean? It sounds serious."

Vem draws in the corners of her wide mouth, a dramatic act for someone with such large lips. "It was the place people visited when the cult disbanded.

Supposed to help them learn how to do basic things in the community. They city thought it would prevent floaters. Everybody who jumps off Piney Falls is a former member of Fallen Branch."

"Who jumps? Like the mayor? Floaters? I heard that term when I checked in to the motel. What information do you have about...?"

"It's almost mid-morning. I have to stay on schedule." She slams the door in my face.

I find the building easily and discover that it is also the tourism center. When I walk in the pristine, white building that looks similar to a bank from the 1930s, I find a tall, marble desk at the far end of this grand room. An elegant woman is perched on a stool, staring intently at the computer screen.

She looks unlike anyone else I've seen in this town. Classy and professional. Bright blue eyes, a perfect oval face and a long, pointed nose. Her hair is shiny; two shades of silver and cut neatly around her face. Her brows are high and thoughtfully sculpted. She is magnificent. I notice she is wearing a bright green nametag, similar to the one the policeman was wearing yesterday. *Welcome to Piney Falls! I'm Cedar! Ask me about our new hot tub!*

When she sees me, she looks up and smiles, displaying straight, bright, white teeth. "Hello and Welcome to Piney Falls! What brings you in today?"

"Lanie Anders." I offer my hand across the counter. She doesn't hesitate and almost pulls me across the counter as she shakes firmly. When she is done, she releases my hand unexpectedly, and it drops with a thud.

"Our community was formerly a known for its logging. Today, you can enjoy hiking, biking, and fishing. John Bower..."

"I already heard about the tours. I'm looking for some information, and I owe you forty-five dollars" I continue. "I'm doing some research on the history of Piney Falls. I was supposed to meet with your mayor, but he..."

She licks her finger before reaching underneath the desk and pulling out several stapled pieces of paper. "These are the handouts we have. If you come in mid-July, you can participate in Aisley Days and the Log Rolling Festival but for now, you can take this walking tour of the town. On the map you'll spot the former Scheddy Cannery location. The new strip mall on the property will open its' first shop soon: Piney Pete's Brewery." She has the smooth speech pattern of those who spend the majority of their time in the business community. We don't bother with emotion.

"No, I'm looking for information on the Flanagans. Whoever it was the town is named after."

Her demeanor instantly changes. Annoyed? "The Scheddys WERE Flanagans. Sisters who went by their maiden names after their husbands died. Most records were lost in a fire. I can't tell you more than what is on the papers I gave you." She is staring at an imaginary something on the ceiling behind me. A common characteristic with people in this town, I'm discovering.

I glance at the plain, typed paper. There are two sentences about the Flanagan sisters. "Is this it? There's nothing on the Internet."

"You've got all the information I have. We don't look back. We keep our gaze pinned toward the future." She smiles, a plastic, creepy smile.

"Where are the city records held then?"

"Burned. Everything burned. Big fire. Like I said." She begins to sketch on one of the extra handouts. Maybe drawing plans for some new architecture. There are lots of squares.

"Cedar —what an unusual name." I try a different angle. "Is that after a relative or something?"

She blinks her beautiful ice-blue eyes. "I grew up in a cult. Zion, the leader, was obsessed with letters. Every kid born the same year had to be named using the same first letter. He had an approved list."

I think about all the stories I've read about cults. Disconnected people. "Where did you grow up?"

"Just outside of town. It didn't start as a cult. He told everyone it was a big commune at first. Wealthy people came from all over the world to learn how to live the Zion Method. It was called Fallen Branch."

I don't know how to react to this news. So, I do what I was taught when I went through HR training; empathize.

"I'm so sorry. You must've gone through so much."

She looks shocked. "Yes, it wasn't a great way to live. Lots of silly rules and Zion got mad about the strangest things. We never saw our parents and spent most of our school time learning stupid lessons Zion thought were important but did nothing to actually teach us how to be adults." She taps one finger on the desk absently. "Sure would have been nice if some adult thought about the kids they created instead of filling their heads with his nonsense."

"How did you escape?"

"He died. Fell off a bridge or something. He was walking back to the compound after a big city council meeting. I'm not really sure. After he was gone, everyone kind of felt free. We all scattered. My parents moved to the East Coast and my brother and I stayed here, making a life for ourselves."

I cluck my tongue and look at her sympathetically. It works. I can see the ice melting from her exquisite face.

She looks around. No one has entered the building since I arrived. "We do have a few things. The day they changed the name from Aisley Lumber Township to Flanagan they took a big group picture."

"Oh, of the two women?"

She shakes her head. "No, of the townies. Sorry, that's a throwback from my cult days. The city officials. This was after the women had jumped over the falls."

"About that—the mayor just died? They told me he jumped too? And that it's a common thing around here?"

She nods. "Sure is. Sure is. Can't tell you why, but

it's been going on for years. Started with the sisters and picked up after Zion's death. Guess they all saw it in the news and decided it was the way to do things."

"Oh, before I forget, here's my fine money." I remove a fifty-dollar bill from my wallet and lay it on the counter. "I had a little mishap yesterday."

"I know. Word travels fast in small towns." She slides the money across the counter and into a drawer. "I don't have change but I can give you credit towards an hour in the city hot tub."

"No, I'm good."

As I head toward the door, I think about all of the deaths that have occurred in this town. Maybe I have another story to write. One that is equally important.

"You know, my twin brother collects old photographs of the area," Cedar call out. "You could go talk to him at Cosmic Cakes and Antiquery. Best pastries on the coast."

I walk three blocks to the bakery. It is a tiny room that contains a strange combination of smells. The delicious aroma of baked goods mixed with the stale smells of a museum. As I continue into the room, I see a doorway into an adjoining space, full of antiques and gift shop items. Below the multi-colored, *Welcome to Piney Falls!* shirts, there are a myriad of antique dishes and children's toys.

A startlingly handsome man emerges from the back room, wiping his hands on his apron. His eyes are just like Cedar's, ice blue. His face is oblong, like hers, but his nose is wide and his smile is warm and engaging. His silver hair is tucked behind his ears, not quite reaching his collar.

"Cosmo Hill. My sister said you would be coming." His voice is deep and smooth, like a late-night radio host.

"Lanie Anders." I shake his hand and he holds it firmly. I sense a heat coming off him. I've seen his type a million times, which is why I feel so irritated he's getting under my skin. "I just left her. She's quick!"

"It's a small town. We like to keep each other apprised of strangers. Would you like an Orion Orange Muffin? Just took a batch out of the oven."

I nod. I didn't bother with breakfast this morning.

"Would you like a coffee? I make a mean latte."

"I've been having withdrawals. Half foam please."

He disappears behind the swinging doors for moment and returns with a plate containing a sugar-coated brown, square muffin that emits an intoxicating, citrusy-cinnamon aroma. In his other hand is an envelope. He guides me to the fourth of five tables with mismatched chairs. Cosmo leaves again and returns a short time later with a cup filled to the brim. Full of foam. "I only know how to do it one way," he explains apologetically.

"Excuse me, ma'am? Do you know you look exactly like a star from the old movies? I can't think of her name." I'm used to the interruptions. It's non-celebrity celebrity.

I look up and feel startled for a moment. She could be my mother. Mid-sixties with a round face and green eyes, like mine. I study her for a minute. She is wearing beige sweats and her curly hair is a swirling mess of grey. Definitely not my mother. Or the woman I last saw two decades ago.

"I know. I get that all the time. Tulip Sloan."

She turns abruptly and walks away with no more conversation. Must be a common trait here. "There was a movie star from the forties." I explain. "She was very popular for a while because her mother forced her to do enough movies to live a lavish lifestyle. She ended up taking her own life. Too much pressure, or too many drugs. You probably already know that story."

He shakes his head. "Never heard of her."

I look down at the coffee and my anxiety starts to rise, but then I remember I'm only here for a short time. I can have coffee, just like everything else, the way I like it when I return to Chicago.

"My sister said you were looking for information on the Flanagan sisters. I can tell you what I know, but it's not much."

I bite into the muffin with a texture more like a donut. Whatever it is, I find it delicious. I notice it has an unusual shape. "Square?" I ask.

Cosmo shrugs. "I hate circles."

He hands me the envelope he's been carrying. I open it to see the first photo, black-and-white of two women. They are both dressed in lacy, calf-length dresses, tightly belted at the waist with wide-brimmed white hats. Both are beautiful women with thick, dark hair, sturdy chins, and deep-set eyes. The one on the left, a scribbling underneath identifies as Fiona, has a slightly squinted gaze. She is taller of the two and looks older. Faye, the other woman identified, has eyes that are wider and doe-like. They both have unruly eyebrows, sharp cheekbones, and heart-shaped faces. The two possess thin lips and long noses. In today's world, they would make millions walking the runway for some overpriced designer. I'd buy four of whatever they modeled in each color.

"They are beautiful women."

Cosmo nods. "Immigrants from Scotland. They married two American brothers and left their sheep farm to come to the U.S. The opportunity arose to run a cannery here, so they all moved from New York."

"The town was named after them? Flanagan was their maiden name, right? How could that be in this time period?"

Cosmo shakes his head. "That I couldn't tell you. I try not to get involved in the politics of things, y'know?"

I don't understand. "But haven't you lived here your whole life?" I push the last bite of his delicious confection into my mouth, wishing there was more. I brush the crumbs away.

"Most of it. I left for about ten years. Had a little distraction. I just don't care. Call it Piney Falls or Flanagan or Beach City. I'm okay with all of it."

I can't hide my frustration. How does he not have the answer to something so simple? How do people live like this? "This is crazy. Someone has to have some information." I begin thinking about what Cedar told me about growing up in a cult, removed from all the normal education.

Cosmo smiles, pulling me in momentarily. He lifts well-defined arms over his head and stretches, and then rubs his face. "Okay; how about this. I'll look through my files and see what else I can find. I keep some historical articles on file in case someone on the antique side of things wants more information." He reaches across the table and brushes the remaining crumbs from my face. "You can stop back in tomorrow sometime."

I'm caught off-guard. No one has ever touched me without my approval. Ever. I've fired people for far less, such as staring at me for more than three seconds. I want to tell him that, but my mouth won't form the words.

"Okay," I say instead. "Is there somewhere else I could look for information? I'm only here a short time."

He cocks his head to the side. "Now that's a shame. I'd love to take you out to Piney Falls. That's the real heartbeat of this area."

I blush, for some odd reason. "Oh, I don't hike. I'm not an outdoorsy type. It looks nice from the pictures I've seen, but probably not my thing."

He shrugs. "Suit yourself. I can tell you're out of kilter. Being next to a waterfall, that's what centers you." He folds his arms across his muscular chest. I'm at once uncomfortable and excited.

"You could always start with the Little Cone. It's

not far and there's a nice area where you can spread a blanket and just stare at the sky while you listen to the falls. That's where folks around here go to tell their deepest darkest secrets. You never know what you might learn."

Dearest Da,

We worked for nearly a year to clear the land for our homesteads. Charles and Albert Todd built us fine homes, overlooking the bay. Almost too grand, if you were asking me. My home has five bedrooms and four floors, counting the attic. Albert Todd, not to be outdone, added a sixth bedroom for his anticipated bounty of bairns.

Now Da, I've not mentioned this delicate matter up 'til now, but it needs saying. Sister Faye is still upset wi' ye. She thought you ought put up a fight when the boys came to ask for our hands. Strangers from Mam's country of origin, how do you know they wouldn't sell us to a trader for a good rum? You were awful trusting, what with us only meeting them twice at the pub. Your only two dochters, she wanted it to be harder to let us go, what with Mam's experience.

I don't fault you, Da. It was Mam's premonition,

and we were all a little shocked when it came to pass. You loved her so; you were eager to see her dreams fulfilled. Sister Faye just wanted reassurance you weren't too eager to rid yourself of her, after what happened. Two less mouths to feed, two less dowries to worry about. Sister Faye's always been one to hold a grudge. She doesn't realize she'll regret this anger someday.

On to more exciting news. It was months before the pier was built and our cannery was fully operational. Sister Faye wished more than once we could bring our strang brothers to help fell the trees, chop them, and paint the cannery. But they are needed on the manas, we are aware.

For months leading up to the opening, we helped the boys make metal cans. We cut pieces of tin formed into a cylinder. We soldered the ends together to make a nice looking can. Then we soldered another round piece on the bottom. The first few, Sister Faye and I stood back to admire our work before our husbands sternly reminded us there was much to be done and little time for pats on the back. We still giggle thinking back to our early days in the business.

We were told all the fish would come in a two-month span. The boys hired thirty of the Chinese men to chop and can the fish. Charles was told they were the hardest workers, though they seemed to enjoy the drink and gambling so readily available. Most of them had to travel here without their families, so there are very few women in this community. There are many fishermen, though the Chinese men aren't allowed to go out in the boats. It's a silly superstition, if you ask me. They are the most intelligent men I've met so far.

Faye and I put labels on the cans but soon we'll hire more men for that. We women want to continue to be at the factory, and we work to make sure the books are done properly, just as you taught us on the manas.

When the cannery finally opened in March, we watched as the little boats went out to sea, sails raised like butterflies on the water. It was a beautiful sight. After a half day, Charles blew the whistle to let the workers, mostly Chinese men, ken that the catch was in.

It is hard, this canning. Not like Mam's canning kitchen where bairns played under her feet and we were finished by day's end. Before an hour was out, the room was filled with the stench of sea life, blood running down the floor in a stream. The Chinese men spoke to each other in a language that sounded angry but their faces didn't convey exasperation, only the serious look of a person hard at work.

Our office, perched above the noisy room, doesn't have glass in the window yet. Despite that, we couldn't hear everything that was said. Mr. Samuel Li, the man we met the first day in town, was working directly below and glanced up at us. Every now and then he would admonish the other men and for a time, they would speak in whispers before becoming animated once more.

When the whistle blew for their afternoon break, Mr. Samuel Li asked for permission to speak with us. His apron was covered in blood so Albert Todd thought it not appropriate but I stepped out in the hall to greet him.

"Great apologies, Missus."

He bowed his head as if he were speaking to royalty. I didn't know why he would apologize.

"Men not used to the presence of ladies. We will not dishonor you again."

Words escaped me. I had no idea what he was talking about. I nodded, and he left the room, ready to eat his meal of dried huckleberries and cured fish.

Charles spoke a little Chinese from all of his travels, so I asked him to find out what was going on. He returned and grinned sheepishly. "The men were cursing in Chinese. They haven't worked in a cannery for a few months, so they are slower than they figure they should be. He promised they wouldn't use profanity in front of you again." It didn't matter so much to me. Kind that he'd care about words spoken I couldn't understand.

Once the salmon was skinned and cut, another metal piece was placed on top. This one with a vent hole. We put those in a vat and boiled them, as we did when Mam canned pears. After they're cooled and dried, Faye and I put on our label.

You remember I had the skill to draw and paint. It drove ya crazy that I preferred my painting to the chores. The tall Hemlock trees make a fine backdrop for my label. The ocean can be a challenge to capture, as its sometimes as angry as an American man with no supper on the table. I finished it off with a black-lettered, "Scheddy's Fine Salmon." I made the background red so as when the cans rust it won't be noticeable, and with a grand fish on the side. Sister Faye and I had to stand and admire the first few of these cans as well.

Mrs. Violet Aisley has been such a help, despite the fact that she is only here part of the year. More than once she's offered her maid to wash our clothes and make us supper on the nights we can't possibly move another muscle after spending the day in the cannery.

Our kind neighbor spends the off season with her bairn in California, two days' train ride. She attends the finest schools and Mrs. Aisley relishes important social events expected of someone like her. Silliness, if you ask me.

I've already told Charles I'll not be doing that. My wee ones are no better than the fresh-faced bairns in Aisley Lumber Township who run in the streets while their families work sun-up 'til sundown. I want them to appreciate an honest day of labor and what it does for the mind and soul.

On the subject of bairns, Sister Faye chases after Wee Hiram. Yes, Da, named after you. He's almost two. Same mop of red, curly hair and devilish, blue eyes, too. If you don't watch him, he finds the best places to hide to keep his mother and aunt hunting for his naughty self all day!

Just a month ago I welcomed my own lovely dochter, named Sarah after our dear mother. She's as sweet as can be, a tuft of soft blonde hair on her head and the greenest eyes. Charles is over the moon. There's no photographer in town, but he promises we'll find our way to Portland soon and all will have our photographs taken.

All is mostly well, Da. Mr. Stanford Aisley, who should be busy running his own lumber yard seems to lurk around the cannery. The boys shoo us away when he comes. I don't trust the man, nor the sour faces the boys seem to have after a meeting with him.

Mr. Samuel Li possesses a wisdom beyond all of us. "Better to light a candle than curse the darkness," he says. He does not smile when he says this, as is usually his manner. Best to follow his sage words.

Your Devoted Dochter,
Fiona Flanagan Scheddy

Chapter Ten

PINEY FALLS, OREGON

Present Day

I find myself once more on Vem's doorstep. As much as I don't want to admit it, I'm fascinated by her. This time she opens the door dressed in all pink, from a fuchsia ribbon in her hair and pink blouse to a pair of uncomfortably tight pink jeans and pink socks. It almost hurts my eyes. She's wearing a different pair of glasses, this time with bright carnation-pink plastic rims.

She bear-hugs me before I can take a step back. "What can I do you for? Back okay?"

It's a completely different Vem than yesterday's dismissive coconut-bra-ed woman. I'm not used to people who display emotion outside of business-fake cheeriness. I fired an assistant once for smiling too much. "My back is perfect, thanks. I have a great mattress. I was wondering if you'd go for a walk with me. I'd like to try a hike to Little Cone."

She looks at me with skepticism. "You could barely make it up those stairs the other day. You sure you want to give this a try?"

I think about Cosmo's impossibly blue eyes. I've never been pulled toward someone like that before. If I don't find the answers I came for, at least I want to make it my goal to see those eyes shining at me at the top of Piney Falls. That's what I decided last night after waking from an inappropriately luscious dream.

"Yes, I do. I've never been one for outdoorsy things. Bugs and nature, unknown elements out of our control...ick. I studied the map and if we go one-quarter mile further each day, I'll be at the top by the end of the week."

She tilts her head. "Umm-hmm. There's no planning these things. Rain. A bad karma day. Let's start out slow. We'll work up to it." She steps toward me, pulling her door shut with a bang. "You wanted to go now, right?"

"Um...of course. You don't want to change out of your nice clothes?" I bought clothes in Chicago especially for outdoor wear. I assumed that's how they do it here."

She shakes her head and we begin walking up the steep hill, stopping every few feet so that I can catch my breath. She pats my back. "Don't worry, Lanie. It gets easier. We'll be at a flat part soon."

I force myself to keep moving, one foot at a time,

trying hard not to curse her for her ability to speak during this challenging walk. Finally, we reach the promised flat ground and I lean against a tree. I can tell she's looking at me out of the corner of her eye. I'm not used to being pitied, but I can't stand up to tell her so. I bet she's not even sweating.

"The thing I missed the most living in California was the smell of these trees. Do you know forests all have a slightly different scent?"

I push on the sides of my face, forcing the dizziness away.

"This forest, smells like history to me. I think about the Flanagan women, here from another country, helping to build the cannery and after that, the hospital. If these trees could talk..."

"Did they live close by?" I look around, trying to picture women in long skirts and uncomfortable shoes, building things, cooking, cleaning, and taking care of children.

"This road was their drive. Over that hill," she points to an even steeper climb, "they lived in one house and the hospital was next door. When you're ready, we can try that hike too."

"What else do you know about them?" I have my breath back and though my legs feel like rubber, I'm not going to let that stop me. "Let's keep going."

"Well, they were hardworking mothers and wives. Until their husbands died, they weren't anything out of the ordinary. For whatever reason, that event made them really BURST out of their shells." She stops to make a rainbow motion with her arms. "Inspirational."

I lean against a moss-covered tree, resting my hands against it. "I can't…I can't…" I look at my pedometer: we've only gone one-eighth of a mile.

"Don't make a habit of that! There're all kinds of critters living on those things! Spiders and creepy crawly bugs of all sorts. You don't know whose home you're destroying!"

I jerk upright, putting my hands on my hips. Panic has set in. There's nothing I can't accomplish inside an office. Out here, I'm lost. "Vem, what do you know about Cosmo and Cedar? From the tourist center and the—"

"A lot. Not much. We grew up together." Her cheery demeanor immediately changes. "Why do you ask?"

"I met them yesterday. Seemed nice enough. They said they grew up in the cult—wait, you grew up in the cult?" Her kind of odd seems out-of-character for what I've read about cults. She's too perky.

She puts her hand in front of my face like she's a stop sign. "We don't talk about Fallen Branch. It's a big secret here."

"Could I just ask you three questions?" *Worm Your Way into Their Hearts with Three Questions; Marketing for the Masses by Marty Hammer.* I slept with him twice during that conference, breaking my own rule about one-and-done encounters.

She cocks her head to the side. "Persistent, aren't

you? Three. That's it. Then we talk about something else."

"What year did Fallen Branch disband?"

Vem holds up one very long finger. "It was in 1996. Right after Zion was killed. He was our leader, we called him Grand Elan, which meant Elk, or so he said. Big imposing guy with bushy eyebrows and a voice that would have been perfect to announce football games. That was the name he used; I never knew if he had a different name in the outside world. You were never allowed to call him Zion to his face. We kids all sat at a long table to eat together, every meal. We shared chores, and the adults took turns teaching us in our little school house in the woods."

We are walking again, much too fast for me but I don't want to stifle the flow of information.

"What...happened...to..." I huff, while trying to drag air into my starving lungs.

"Two." She makes a peace sign with her fingers. "I was probably four or five when I realized everyone born the same year as me had an "N" name. Nora, Natalie, Norm, Nial. It was Zion's command. He would see the letter in a vision before the beginning of the new year, Zion's new year, in August. He was absolutely obsessed with the alphabet and order, but strangely never the alphabet in order. Before my sixth birthday, he had us sitting alphabetically by our first name letter. My parents finally realized he was crazy after that. They thought they joined a commune, not a crazy man's fantasy. It took them more than a decade to get out; it was only when he died that they found the courage to leave."

I stop, unable to keep up the pace and bend over, willing myself to stay alert. When I can think again, I wonder about Cedar and Cosmo, living like zombies with no free thought.

"I'm so sorry for the childhood you had. I can relate to feeling like you had no control over your life. I was miserable too. If you—"

"Three." She has three fingers in the air and has begun walking again without asking if I'm ready to move. I'm not.

"It was even more traumatic when we left. I had no experience with other people, or trying to fit in with the normal world. We moved into town. The people here didn't know what to think of us, and the kids still in the cult wouldn't have anything to do with us either. We didn't know if we were supposed to stay with our remaining group members or if we should try to integrate into the community. Between us, the kids, we were stuck too. You know what happened to my... the mayor. He was former Fallen Branch. Cedar had been one of my closest friends for years, but when it ended, so did our relationships. There was some ugliness. Never spoke again. For obvious reasons."

Not obvious. I put my hands on my waist. I'm definitely done for today. "I just need one more answer. Consider it a loan toward tomorrow's questions: What happened to Zion?"

She stares at me like I'm speaking a foreign

language. I give up. There's only so much I can do when my legs are barely underneath me and my chest feels like it might explode. I look around and see a well-worn path to our left. "This is enough for me today. I'm going to head back, maybe take this shortcut."

Vem lets out a loud howl. Startled, I turn around and stare at this pink-clad woman, fists clenched, staring at the sky. I can't help myself. I begin to laugh.

"I'm so sorry. This— you— this place; everything is just...bizarre." Now there is more laughter until it turns into tears running down my face. I don't know quite what's come over me. Maybe this is how people end up disoriented and dead in the forest: exhaustion. Vem pauses for a moment before joining me. She honks like a goose until tears pour out of her eyes, too.

I sit down on the ground, right where I am, body completely spent. I can't remember any other time in my life when I willingly sat on the ground. Whatever crawls or slithers in this area may consume me at any minute, or I may have killed an entire village of ants, but I don't care.

Vem moves in close, folding at the waist and pulls a chunk of frizzy hair away from her eyes. She looks at my face with concern. "Are you okay? Normal people don't just plop down in the middle of the forest like that. Do you know what kind of insect life you could decimate? Seems you've got a little of the bizarre in you, too."

I blink slowly, trying to focus on her face. When I'm ready to stand, she pulls me up. I take care not to bump her head as I let the blood flow back into my scalp. I'm not ok. I lost everything I owned. I don't know who I am without possessions or a job. "You're right. Nobody is completely normal." I think about my weeks on Dancinee's couch. And that totally inappropriate night before.

"What if I ask you about the place you grew up and I don't call it anything? Just childhood memories that changed when a man fell over a bridge?"

"NO MORE QUESTIONS," she mouths. "Two things, Lanie," she says out loud. "First, I don't want to talk about my time there. Remember, I told you we don't talk about Fallen Branch? And second, Zion didn't fall over a bridge. He was murdered. By Cosmo."

Chapter Eleven

AISLING LUMBER TOWNSHIP

Dearest Da,

Things are worse here than I ever thought possible. A horrible death overtook our wee town. We lost seven workers at the cannery. One of my favorites, Mr. McBard, was the first to go. He always bowed and greeted me as if I were a queen. I think Mr. Samuel Li demanded it of him, as he does of all the employees. He really should be foreman, but Charles says it isn't right to put a Chinese man in charge.

We shared stories of our homelands when we took a break from our jobs. He had a wife and son back in Ireland and hoped to bring them to Aisley Lumber Township soon. He saved every penny he made, never gambling like most men do in their off hours. We created a school in our home for any children who wanted to attend and I promised that his son would be able to sit with Sarah and Wee Hiram.

That happened a mere two weeks ago. One day, as we walked out on the pier during our lunch, he told me he felt ill. I touched his head for fever and it was as hot as bread fresh from the oven. As soon as Charles came home, he pulled me aside and said several at the lumber mill had already died of the illness, known to be the Spanish Flu. He didn't want Sarah around the death, so I sent her to the cold bedroom on the top floor with her nanny. They stoked the fire and used all of our blankets.

Each warker turns to his own culture's potions and remedies when illness strikes. We have no doctor here in our little cove to tell them different. I invited Mr. McBard, being alone in this remote village, into our home where we placed a cot in the sun room for his care. I covered his head in wet cloths soaked in lavender water. Mr. Samuel Li brought green tea and special herbs. The Irish men came with a warm whiskey and cloves mixture. The Norwegians brought Aquavit; an alcohol made from potatoes. Each group assured their methods would cure anything. All seemed successful for a time but in the end, they were no match for this mighty foe.

Soon, spots appeared on his cheeks. Charles asked me to leave the room but I couldn't bear to leave my friend's side. I held his hand and closed my eyes as he struggled to breathe. He tried mightily to grasp enough air to survive. None of the remedies brought him relief. His chest rose less and less and then the room was filled with silence. I wished him to take one raspier gasp, staying in our world just a few minutes more.

Charles and another warker took him out in a boat and buried him at sea. Mr. McBard loved being on the water. It was best to do; we feared burying our dead on land when there were so many. No time to feel sadness for this loss. More pressing to me, the safety of the new life inside me and keeping Sarah healthy.

Charles and his brother decided it would be best to shut down the cannery for a few weeks, to ensure no more workers became ill. It was too late though, as we would lose another five to the flu before the end of it.

The following week we were awoken by the sound of Alfred Todd, banging furiously on our door. Wee Hiram had taken ill.

Poor sweet thing. His body contorted with pain, trying to breathe in his mother's arms as she smothered his chest in a mustard poultice. The normally rambunctious youngster became lethargic and didn't fight his mother's comfort. She held him day and night and finally we decided the time had come to take him to Portland. Being young and strang, we hoped for his survival with the care of trained doctors.

We all got on the train, leaving Sarah behind with her nanny. Sister Faye hadn't slept since her son took ill and Alfred Todd was wild with worry, unable to make a decision on his own. I was tired from trying to nurse all the sick men and didn't want to leave my own child, but I knew Faye needed me more.

There was such a scare over the flu that those with

even a hint of illness weren't allowed to board the train. Faye wrapped Wee Hiram up tightly and held him close to her chest, telling him not to cough until the conductor had passed. By some miracle, he kept silent until we took our seats at the back and the train had left the station. Charles held his coat up high so others couldn't see the boy's ashen face and cause a panic. When his arms tired, it was my turn.

Wee Hiram slept in his mother's arms most of the way, his lungs rattling so loud at times we heard them above the roar of the train. We were just outside of town when I noticed the spots on his cheeks, just like Mr. McBard's. My heart sank. We hurried to the hospital, four blocks from the station. I knew we weren't going to make it in time, but I dared not say it out loud. After Mr. McBard I cared for six more men who died shortly after developing the spots on their cheeks. By the time we reached the hospital, my sweet nephew had gone to be with his sainted grandmother, his gentle face no longer contorted with pain.

The hospital wouldn't allow us to take the bairn home for proper burial. They said the sickness was too strang, even in a body that wasn't among the living. Charles wired Mr. Stanford Aisley, who promised he would make arrangements for our red-headed love to be returned to Aisley Lumber Township immediately, rules be damned. Sure enough, his defeated form arrived two days later in the back of a well-paid farmer's wagon.

Sister Faye was beside herself. She wanted him

buried in the woods behind our homes, an area we worked so hard to clear to plant our fields of vegetables. The cemetery was full of grown men and a few prostitutes, she said. Wee Hiram loved to chase his dog around outside, sometimes disappearing in the woods for hours until Sister Faye threatened to withhold his supper.

Instead, we decided to have our own service on our hill, Scheddy Hill. We could still plant our crops and Wee Hiram could watch from his perch above us. Mr. Stanford Aisley made him a nice cross from Hemlock wood. Mrs. Aisley played a moving, American song, "Farewell My Prince," on her fiddle. Our dear boy was, after all, an American boy. Her smooth thoughtful song brought more tears to my eyes, tears I didn't think still existed. Reminded me of the day we put Mam in the earth. Do you remember, Da? You insisted the preacher lead everyone in a silly, American tune. Was it Yankee Doodle?

Sister Faye didn't shed one tear. I don't think she had anything left in her, either. She stood, unblinking, through the whole thing. Like one of Sarah's porcelain dolls.

By the end of it all, we'd lost nearly sixty in our community. The madams were hit particularly hard. Now Da, you always said not to judge a profession as it was a way to put food in the mouths of the babes. Some of these poor women came here thinking they'd be quick to find a husband.

The Chinese women tugged at my heart. Arriving

here with high hopes and expectations of finding their own Charles or Albert Todd, they were instead forced into prostitution just to eat. Their pretty brown eyes didn't possess the same sparkle as Mr. Samuel Li's. I wished them happiness when I saw them. Now, many of those delicate souls are gone.

As you can imagine, Sister Faye is nothing but a shell of herself. It's been almost two months now and the poor lass can't even take in a walk to the Falls without falling to her knees. The birth of my second bairn, Walter, cheered her for a day and then she was back to her sullen ways. She's got a small one at home, Percival, who needs caring for. Along with our jobs at the cannery, and keeping the fields weeded, we don't have time for the sorrow that hangs like a thick cloud over our mountain.

Your Devoted Dochter,
Fiona Flanagan Scheddy

Chapter Twelve

CHICAGO, ILLINOIS

2018 - Two Weeks Ago

"**N**o offense, Lanie, but this has gotten kinda weird."

Dancinee pulls her hair up tight on top of her head and stares in the mirror while she talks to me, the interloper who has been on her couch for three weeks.

"I mean, you're a rich lady with lots of resources. Don't your fancy friends have extra houses? You could always ask one of them if you would be able to stay in their guest chall-let or something."

"Chalet." There is no logical reason for me to be camping out in the living room of someone I barely know. Although she always refuses, I've offered to compensate her generously for my presence. "You're right though. I don't know why I haven't been able to pull things together." I can't even bring myself to go into work, the place that felt more familiar than my knick-knack consumed showpiece of a home.

"Your insurance agent came by the casino again," she sprays some foul-smelling hairspray all around her head. I make a mental note to purchase a nice hair product for her. Whenever it is that I can get off the couch.

"It's really weird, if you ask me. How would he have any idea where to find me? And why is he bothering me? Getting up in my business like he's my crazy uncle or something. You need to call him back. Today." She grabs her keys from the kitchen counter and walks to the door, pausing to stare at me. "Are you hearin' me? That's all you have to do today, Lanie. Call that creep and tell him to quit stalking me. Oh, and quit rearranging my cupboards. They are fine as is. Just like my calendar, and my drawers... Are you seeing a pattern? Maybe two things. Call the creep and go for a walk. You've been complaining about my coffee and the lack of milk."

"Foam. Half-foam latte. It's my usual and—"

"I know. You've got order in your life. I haven't forgotten. Except there's no order to camping in my living room."

I nod. I need to do this for her and quit wallowing in my...whatever it is. I've given her phone number to everyone involved in restoring my home, something I neglected to mention. Another strange piece to my new personality.

"'Kay then." She's got her public voice on. "See you tonight!" She doesn't wait for me to respond.

I pause for a moment, sinking back into my misery. Unable to function, trying to control the life of someone who didn't ask to be my landing spot. I'm pathetic. I scroll through my messages and find the five left by Bentley, the insurance agent. I hate people named Bentley. There is one underneath, from a number I don't recognize. So sorry to hear about your house. Please let me know if I can be of any help. Carl

I search my brain, trying to figure out how this person has my number. Most of the time, I give out my business phone so I can turn it off at night. Then it comes to me. It's my teacher from that silly creative writing course. The one I carelessly took to my room the night of the fire. Cosmically, that fire must've been my punishment for being with him.

Now that I've had some time to think, I wonder why I have to sleep with everyone, including him. I think about the bad days I've had. Maybe they are all connected to these one-night stands.

Thanks. I appreciate your concern.

I'll give him credit for trying.

Can we meet for lunch?

If I meet with him, I'll apologize and start getting my life back. Things will go back to the way they should be.

I shower, horrified at the image in the mirror. I

sent Dancinee out to purchase toiletries for me but she came back with cheap products that don't take kindly to my face. I'm puffy and old looking. Like someone without a sense of purpose in their life.

After putting on the black stretch slacks Dancinee's mother brought me and the one green silk blouse that survived in my overnight bag, I forego looking in the mirror again before walking out the door.

I find the Tac-o-the-Townies taco truck and wait, trying to avoid the gaze of those around me. I must look like I've been working the night shift. When he arrives, I find his appearance much more pleasing than I remembered. Handsome, in a limited sense. My metrics for attractiveness are usually based on availability and lack of a wedding ring, but I was drunk. I stare at his finger. No ring.

"Lanie, I'm so glad you called. I've been worried about you. We miss you in class." He kisses my cheek and touches my back lightly. He smells slightly of body odor and coffee. We order our lunch and sit on a park bench nearby.

"I don't know why I called you. I don't know why I do anything right now, to be honest." I force a smile.

"Can I be blunt with you?"

Whenever someone says that to you in the business world, that means you're either fired or they're having a crappy day and they want to release their life story into your lap.

"I think you're in a funk because you've never been on the bottom before."

"I'm the hardest worker you'll find. I patterned my life after the actress Tulip Sloan. She never turned down paying gigs; made thirty movies in five years. My body of work speaks for itself. I'm number one in my field. I put in seventy-hour work weeks. That's what it takes to succeed."

He puts his hand up. "Let me explain. I've had students like you before. They sit in the front row, eagerly answer every question, and turn in their work on time using the exact word count I ask for. The perfect students." He crumples his taco wrapper and shoots it into the adjacent trash can. It bounces on the rim and lands at my feet.

I pick it up and shoot it in myself. A perfect shot.

"These students are impeccable," he continues, "until something out of their control happens. Perhaps they had a family issue or big shake up at work that didn't allow them to finish the project on time. Their world just crumbles. They don't understand how to fail."

If I were able to work up the energy, I would be furious with this stupid, little man. "So, you think I don't understand how to fail? I assure you I've had plenty of failure before. I dust myself off and keep going."

"But you could control the outcome, right? Go back and re-do a project, work with a client to make it better. There has always been a path to success in what-ever you're doing. It's things out of your control, like, say, nature, or a fire that really throw you for a loop."

I think about that for a minute. I don't do much in nature because I don't like to worry about what will happen if the elements take over. What if it rains or snows? I like the comfort and structure of my home. The men I sleep with are all a well-orchestrated end to the conferences I attend.

"You're probably right, as much as I hate to admit it. I hired the best contractor. I've done remodels before and never had any issues. Starting over with my—"

"Your identity. Your house was your identity. That's what you told me that night when we..." He is bright red. He must not make a habit of this the way I do.

"So, what do you think I should do with myself, Carl?"

Carl leans back against the bench and pulls his sunglasses out of his jacket pocket. Though they are obviously cheap, they give him a rugged appearance. Almost appealing. It appears I've been sequestered for too long.

"Dancinee says you've taken a leave of absence from work. It might be a good idea to get away and press your restart button. See life from another perspective. Go somewhere you've never been. You know, you never turned in your project." He turns to me and smiles. "A road trip to Piney Falls might be in order."

I think back to that night, and the story I was planning to write about murder and intrigue in a small town. "Oh, I couldn't find any information."

"People act differently when you meet them face-to-face. You could write something fictional, as was your assignment. Or, you could dig deep, find out what really happened. It could be that they are like you: finding a new identity because something tragic happened to their old one."

A vacation. Not a furniture-buying venture. If I'm being honest, a lot of that was expected in my social circle. Something completely unexpected might be just what I need.

"That's brilliant, actually. Something to get my mind off my house. It will take a while before I can rebuild. I don't need to sit around and wallow in depression watching that every day. Thank you, Carl!" This will make Dancinee so happy. I've made a break-through. And this taco, as much as I hate to admit it, tastes pretty good.

"You're welcome, Lanie." He takes a deep breath. "Now, should we talk about what happened? Between the two of us?"

"Yes, that's really why I agreed to meet you. I wanted to apologize for treating you the way I did. I'll be honest, I've had many one-night – 'adventures' - let's call them. Business acquaintances. It is a very disciplined evening. I know what to say, when to ask them to leave. It's much easier that way, for both of us, I'd imagine. This is the first time I've been with someone I might encounter again."

"Oh, one of those." He puts his hands in his jacket pockets.

"You're a lovely man. I'm just not good at relationships."

"If you don't ever allow yourself to be a little vulnerable, you'll never experience a real relationship. Be open to someone who doesn't fit that mold and you might be surprised what happens. I had ten great years with a wonderful woman because I allowed myself to fall and get back up again."

I want to protest but I can feel it in my gut: he's right. Again.

"What happened? You said ten years?"

He stands up and buttons his suit jacket. "She decided she wanted to travel the world. I didn't. We learned to communicate well, even when it meant saying good bye."

"You deserve to find another someone." I wish I wouldn't have made fun of him.

"I've got a Roman Literature class in ten minutes. I do wish you the best, Lanie."

As he walks away, I call after him, "Thanks! For all of your help!" There is a sliver of guilt that I push away.

I sit for another hour, making plans. I can sense myself slipping into my work mode again and it feels like putting on a comfortable pair of shoes. The cool breeze invigorates me while I make a spread sheet, not an easy fete to accomplish on my phone. The finished product details my travel itinerary and all the contact information.

By the time Dancinee comes home from work that evening, I've bought myself a suitcase and enough clothing to last me a month. I've cleaned her apartment with all the half-empty bottles of cleaning supplies I could find and ordered out for dinner; Jack's Chicken Shack, her favorite. I only re-organized one more cupboard, the one above her sink that really needs to include dish soap. Things are settled with Work Ahead Office Supplies - The Most Profitable Office Supply Chain in the World.

"You're dressed! I'll have to call my mom and pay up. She bet me it would take another month!"

She kicks her shoes off and walks to the kitchen, but I block her from entering. "There's more to tell your mom. I've washed her clothes and bought some of my own. I rented a car, planned a route and tomorrow I'm taking off."

She looks at me with shock. "Not Europe? Is there a lamp in Italy that needs you?"

"God, you make me sound pretentious. I suppose I am. I'm truly sorry for that."

I pull a new, plaid placemat from the cupboard next to the plates, where I thought it belonged. I set it on the table and take the foil off her chicken wings and put them on a plate on the bar that separates the kitchen from the living room that has doubled as the bedroom of a very confused woman for the past three weeks.

"Go ahead and sit down." I motion to the table where I've placed fresh orange daisies in a vase I found at the boutique across from my favorite clothing store. "I had a conversation with Carl today. I'm going to take an adventure to Piney Falls. "

"That place from your assignment? Is that a vacation spot for rich people? I always thought you liked islands and places with names the rest of us couldn't pronounce."

"Oh Dancinee. Didn't you know we can make anything comfortable with the right luggage?" I laugh a fake laugh, hoping she'll join in. She doesn't. "This time I'm going to venture out a little. See things from a different perspective. I want to figure out why this little town needed to change its identity."

She eyes me suspiciously. "You're not on something, right? I wouldn't feel good about letting you leave if you had some kind fancy drug in your system."

I pat her back. "No, dear. You don't have to worry. This will be good. It's really just what I need."

The next morning, I leave ten crisp, one-hundred-dollar bills on her dresser, offering suggestions for their use. A good coffee maker would make her mornings so much easier. There are five more gentle nudges on the list. Also included is a note with the address of the house I've rented and the name of my architect and contractor, who've been given her contact information, along with the insurance agent who has been bothering her. She'll be annoyed I gave her number to yet another person.

After driving across the country for three days, seeing rolling hills, massive thunder clouds and tall green crops, I reach the northern coast of Oregon. I'm in awe of the straight evergreen trees that seem to touch the sky. They cover the mountainous landscape in a thick blanket. When I break into the open space, the valleys are lush and green, giving way to small creeks and rivers. I pass clumps of tall, thin deciduous trees before climbing hills again. When I reach the coastline, the blue ocean borders me on one side while the rugged landscape of tall trees fills my view on the other side. It is at once terrifying and thrilling. There are large rocks jutting from the ocean here and there, using their own pattern to display nature's exotic beauty.

I'm exhausted after my drive, but finally, as the sun is dipping behind what seems like the edge of the earth tucked into a corner of the ocean, I see a wooden carved sign beside the road. *Welcome to Piney Falls! Established 1988.* I roll down my window, hoping to hear ocean sounds but instead there is a deafening quiet. No cars driving by or the bustling noises of people living their lives that I'm used to in the big city.

I can smell the light, salt air, though. It comes into my nostrils and travels through my body, overtaking weeks of tension with peace and instilling a sense of calm. This is where I belong.

Chapter Thirteen

PINEY FALLS, OREGON

Present Day

"Thanks for the photos." I avoid his gaze.

"Did something change?" he asks, setting an unwanted mug of coffee with frothy milk in front of me and pulling up a chair. I can smell brownies baking. It's hard to be upset with someone who is baking brownies.

"I don't know what you mean." I take a sip and then a bite of the Pegasus Peach Marionberry Muffin, square of course, he set on the table as well. I stare at the plastic, red-checkered table cloth.

"Well, yesterday I felt a vibe between us. An energy of some kind. Today you're as cold as the January rain. There has to be a reason for that."

Is it worth it? I'm just here for a month at most, trying to write a story that doesn't seem to matter anymore. I don't need to hear this guy's whole life story.

"My neighbor, Vem, November, tells me you've had a colorful life." I take a sip. Another bite.

"Good ol' November. I heard she was back. Hasn't had the guts to come in here and see me. But I shouldn't be surprised. She always thought she was better than me and Cedar."

"The way she tells it, you two were the ones who shunned her. She also told me about your incarceration."

I take this opportunity to study his perfectly smooth face. That must be why it's as flawless as slow-motion buttermilk poured from a pitcher: He never saw daylight. He frowns and looks out the small window above my head. "Yeah, that's true. Ten years for murder. November's got to make sure everyone knows I'm evil."

There is a vulnerability in his voice. I realize how petty and gossipy I sound. Whatever this feud is about rests squarely between the three of them. As much as I'm trying to change, it is coming in small starts. "I'm sorry. It's really none of my business. You've obviously turned your life around and that's all that matters."

He snorts. "'Turned it around.' I guess so. Did she tell you why I was incarcerated?"

"No," I lie. "It's not my business. You don't have to—"

"Murder. I was in prison for killing the leader of our commune, Zion."

I'm not quite sure how to respond. "I'm sure he deserved it," I say quietly.

"More than you know. I hated him for splitting up our family and all the others in the compound. We never really knew our parents. None of us — kids or adults —understood how to function without him, which is exactly how he wanted it. He was a monster."

His passion surprises me. "I won't ask you any more about this." I'm dying to learn more. "I'm sorry I brought it up. I'm here to learn about the Flanagan sisters and that's where we should really focus our time and energy, don't you think?"

"Suit yourself."

There's another envelope on the table today. I pull it towards me and take out the contents. Whether they are interesting or not, I'll find a way to segue to this conversation.

"I found more stuff. Thought you would be interested."

There are three articles: one about the Scheddy Salmon Cannery, one about the giant lumber mill and one about the naming of the town of Flanagan. There are more pictures too. I recognize the women from yesterday's photos.

"That's Faye Scheddy." He points to a picture of a family, the diminutive woman with large dreamy eyes standing next to a lanky man who looks like he's drunk. His eyes are half-open and he's leaning on a chair in front of him. There are two boys sitting cross legged on the floor. They look like their mother. I study Faye's face; she looks incredibly sad.

I move to the next picture, Fiona, a taller and more

serious-looking woman. She is sitting erect in the same chair and her husband is sitting next to her. There is a small table between them and both of their hands are resting there, touching, just barely. "They're smiling," I point out, hoping this will change topics sufficiently. "That's unusual for photos from this time period."

"Definitely two different stories." Cosmo stands up and pours himself a cup of coffee.

I stare at the children in the second photo. A daughter with the same pointed, precise features as her father stands behind him with her hand resting on his shoulder. Self-assured and smiling. She is stunning. There are three more boys sitting on the floor, almost identical to the boys in the other photo. I put them side by side just to make sure they aren't the same.

"Names are on the back, if that's what you were wondering."

"This is all going to be very helpful with my research. I promise to bring everything back tomorrow."

"If you're sure being seen with a felon another day won't cause you too much trauma." Cosmo smiles that disarming smile.

I blush. *Dammit.* Blushing is for naïve young girls. "What you did isn't any of my concern, really. I just waltzed into your life looking for something else and I... Thank you for finding this for me. I would appreciate any further information." I stand up even though I haven't finished my coffee — the same cup I didn't want but now can't put down. There is nothing but crumbs left on my square plate. I can't allow things to get awkward between us.

When I get to the door, I stop and turn around. "I went out into nature yesterday," I blurt. There is an elderly gentleman looking at antiques in the other room who pokes his head around the corner. He's probably never actually seen someone of my species before.

"Good for you, Lanie. Good for you. Keep working on it and we'll be able to take that hike to Piney Falls before you go. If you're still interested." Cosmo gives me the 'thumbs up' sign. I don't understand why that means so much to me.

I walk outside the door and stand for a moment. Impulsively, I walk back in. "I'm not afraid of you," I announce. The man from the other room walks back in.

Cosmo has the cash register open, counting change. He doesn't look up. "That's good. I'm not a dangerous guy, unless you cross my family. You'll be relieved to learn I'm not afraid of you either. Perhaps a little intrigued."

I want to sit back down and ask a million questions about Cosmo Hill. Instead, I turn and leave.

Chapter Fourteen

AISLEY LUMBER TOWNSHIP, OREGON

Dearest Da,

The fever that struck our town is a dark memory never to be spoken of again. We don't have to speak of it, the damage to our little family isn't likely to fade.

Sister Faye is no longer herself. Her smile has gone from her eyes; I fear it has permanently disappeared. She's given birth to her third bairn, second living, and she barely notices the poor boy exists. My Sarah cheerfully tends to baby Padrug and the other boys, Faye's and two of mine. Faye won't allow the nanny, or anyone outside the family access to her home.

Sister Faye goes about her duties without thought, milking cows and tending the garden each morning. She barely speaks to Alfred Todd, and he seems to be little more aware of her presence. Mrs. Aisley felt it might be better for Faye to winter in San Francisco to remove herself from these memories. She shook her head no until we thought it would fall off her shoulders. I was secretly glad we would be staying. My bairns don't need a fancy life, just an honest one.

Though Charles is gone for months at a time adventuring across the country with his brother, he loves his children, especially Sarah. He has a fondness for her gentle way and a great respect for her intelligence. He says someday she'll become a scholar and make the world a better place.

I'm glad I can confide in you, Da. With Sister Faye so distant, the only other woman close to me is Mrs. Aisley. Though she can be a great comfort, there is something I still don't trust about her. She has a hunger to gain the secrets of others and a desire to share them with whoever she has in her parlor during tea time.

During one such visit, I witnessed her sharing the story of poor Mrs. Winthrop. Though her son, Jasper, attends the finest schools in San Francisco, he's yet to master writing a decent paper. Mrs. Winthrop hired tutors who quit in exasperation. She began to do the boy's schoolwark on her own.

As Mrs. Aisley explained the Winthrop's humiliation over being kicked out of the academy named after their family, she seemed to forget poor Mrs. Winthrop was seated on the blue-striped settee right behind her.

My trust is in shorter supply yet with Mr. Stanford Aisley. He, himself is quite aware of the heartache he causes those around him, especially those in his employ. I daresay his wife isn't treated much better.

She reveals stories of his dismissal of her and their bairn, who knows him only by name, and is to be unseen in his home. He is out most evenings, not reading sweet tales to them as they drift off to sleep, Mrs. Aisley unsure of his whereabouts.

A recent story regarding him is especially unsettling. The ocean so often appears calm and lovely, though there are hidden dangers. The water is frequently full of logs. Those of us who cleared land close to the water were able to roll the beasts into the water. Those further away were not so lucky, starting their logs on fire and sometimes their homes as well. When these timbers crash to shore, they crush any human unlucky enough to be in the way.

Out at sea things are just the same. Large waves can come out of nowhere and overturn a small fishing boat in one surge of power. Because of this, logs aren't the only danger to those unsuspecting souls walking the beach. Bodies are a common sight, in between logs or on their own. That is just what happened to this poor chap, the foreman at the lumber mill. A giant wave overtook his fishing boat.

The bairns love playing on the beach, frolicking no matter the time of year. They have no sense of the dangers approaching and many mornings are caught in a sudden surge of sea, waves crashing up close to shore. Usually an adult is nearby, but sometimes parents are too busy and shoo their young off to play alone.

When this body washed ashore, as many do, Da, some German children found him. They came to the cannery and asked for me. I believe they were frightened to approach any of the men, who carried big knives and speak harshly in other tongues throughout the course of their demanding job.

I knew what we would find, so I wasn't afraid. I've seen many a dead since Mam's passing. Sometimes one or more a week. It's a hard life here.

When I followed the children, I found a short, stout man with no beard. Mr. Stanford Aisley didn't allow men with facial hair to work for him, no matter the position. This poor soul was wearing the dark blue shirt and pants required as uniform for Aisley Lumber Mill and a long oil coat. His scuffed gum boots were like those of any fisherman. A light blue handkerchief, also company issue, was in the chest pocket. I further examined his body to find it clean of wounds until I turned him over. On the back of his head was a large, gaping hole, splinters of wood still stuck in the wound caused by hitting his head on the boat, no doubt.

When I went to the lumber mill to tell Mr. Stanford Aisley, describing his foreman in great detail, he asked if I was sure of the identity of the man. I was. He waved his hand and said, "Tell my men to bury the lout at high tide." With that, he called another man into his office and declared him foreman, continuing his paperwark.

"Don't you want to write a letter to his family?" I asked hopefully.

"No," he said. "I don't busy myself with trivial

matters. They'll figure it out when they stop receiving money."

As heartless as this incident was, I can give you an even more startling example. Last month, one of the men was out scouting the waters for lost souls. Sometimes men will go, out of the goodness of their hearts, searching for those who misjudged the rough sea. This kind soul was around Headache Point, thusly named for the trouble it causes those who believe they can maneuver the tricky bit of ocean and land in any kind of weather. Days later, he washed ashore along with pieces of one of Mr. Stanford Aisley's small boats.

Mr. Stanford Aisley declared him a fool and immediately charged the man's family for the price of the boat and the day's wages lost.

Mr. Samuel Li witnessed this exchange and motioned for me to join him outside. He disclosed that he distrusts the man just as I do. He looked me in the eye and told me Mr. Stanford Aisley is drunk with himself, a condition that will cause him a violent end.

He seems to have a keen sense of the future, beginning with our first encounter on the mountain when he guided us to the very spot where we built our homes. I told him how I'm concerned about Charles and Albert Todd spending so much time in the company of such a man. "If your problem has no solution, then why worry about it?" He asked wisely. But I do, I insisted. I have a bad sense in my body about what will come next. Mr. Stanford Aisley is evil and Charles is oblivious to his sharp edges.

Mr. Samuel Li shook his head. "Worry only robs you of today. Let me carry that burden on my back. When the time comes, I return the load gently. By then, you'll be strong enough to bear its contents."

Something about him both comforts and terrifies me.

Your Devoted Dochter,
Fiona Flanagan Scheddy

Over a dinner of squash and roasted chicken, I stare at the vastness of the ocean, trying to imagine what it might have been like when the Flanagan sisters arrived. A brutal, unforgiving environment with little to offer women of the time. It must've been oppressive.

The envelope from Cosmo is sitting on the table. What a complicated man. I've never been drawn to someone so urgently before. *Stop it, Lanie. He's not a marketing seminar conquest.* It's best to focus on the information in front of me.

The first article is about the anniversary of the Scheddy Salmon Cannery. The women and their husbands are standing in aprons in front of the building. No one looks particularly happy to be there. A tiny, stern-looking man wearing a tall hat stands in front of them. There is an Asian man standing behind them holding a bucket. "Scheddy Salmon Cannery and Aisley Lumber Mill work in harmony for five years. Cannery workers spend their off-season working at the lumber mill, keeping the town thriving."

The next one is dated almost fifteen years later. "Founder of Aisley Lumber Mill and Aisley Lumber Township Killed in Cannery Fire." Mr. Stanford Aisley, owner of six buildings and the foundation of our community, died in a tragic fire yesterday. According to Mr. Samuel Li, cannery and lumber mill employee, Mr. Stanford Aisley often drank as he did the bookwork late into the night. He passed out and knocked over his kerosene lantern, which caused the fire.

The next morning before I've even had my breakfast, there is a knock on the door. It is Vem. She's dressed entirely in orange today. With her pale complexion, she reminds me of a construction cone. "We're going to try again. We will make it to the top of Little Cone. I won't give up on you."

I sigh. Yesterday's excitement has waned. I haven't put together a plan for a new hike. I'd rather sit on the couch and drink my coffee, trying to put these pieces together. "I'm not sure I'm in the mood today."

She stands immobile. "We're going. If you get nothing else from this vacation, you'll learn how to hike."

"I'm usually the one giving out the orders," I say weakly. She doesn't respond.

Grudgingly, I pull on my sneakers and slip my arms through the sleeves of my new turquoise fleece coat with a Scenic Piney Falls patch on the front. I found it in the closet with a "my gift to you" note attached. I pull my hair back in a ponytail. As I look in the mirror, I realize I've forgotten to put on my makeup every day I've been here. "I've gained at least five pounds from those square pastries at Cosmo's Bakery," I say out loud. "Sorry, I don't mean to offend you by bringing up his name."

"We've all got our quirks from our years in Fallen Branch." Vem smiles. "Square foods are his. I laughed when I read the description of his little bakery. 'Full of cosmic goodness in square formation.' So Cosmo."

And matching outfits are yours.

"I won't bring him up again. I'll keep my dirty bakery secrets to myself from now on."

"I made a mistake. He's still upset. That's all there is to say." She stretches her arms over her head. "Hurry up."

"What brought you back here, Vem? It sounds like you didn't have happy memories growing up. Why did you return?" I set the alarm on my phone. If I don't have a plan, at least I'll time our walk. To keep myself on track.

As we head up the path, Vem takes my hand. She stares intently into my eyes, making me very uncomfortable. "You deserve to know. You came here for answers," she says, squeezing my palm tightly.

"Yes, I did." As little as I wanted to exercise, I want it even less if it will involve hand-holding. I want to turn around and go back home, but I need to stay on schedule. If nothing else, I'll get that part of my life back in this little town. I continue walking, my hand tightly in her grasp.

"It seemed familiar. I married the first person to be nice to me. It was as simple as that. I didn't know how to weed out the bad people because we had to trust everyone in Fallen Branch and outsiders were all bad. The townies thought we were all bad. They kept a list of all former Fallen Branch members in town and kept a close watch. You can see how a guy with a friendly smile was all I needed." She is squeezing my hand uncomfortably tight. I attempt to wiggle my fingers, trying to keep circulation.

"My husband and I moved right away, and I was lost. I spent all of those years in California, never seeing a familiar face. I needed something that felt like normal, you know?"

She continues to cling tightly to me. Once we get to the steep part, I'll need both of my arms for momentum. "You wanted something comforting."

"Yes, comforting. My husband was abusive. So many years I just took it. That's what my childhood taught me. No matter how ghastly things become, you shut up and take it."

I think about the world I came from. The world I knew growing up. "My mother was very controlling. She had this child who looked like a movie star and she used it to get whatever she wanted. She forced me to sign autographs in the mall as Tulip Sloan, even though the woman was long dead. I had to walk and talk just like she wanted because if I didn't, it would be my fault we weren't bringing in money. I never played with friends or did anything normal." I take a deep breath. "Now, I'm always in control - from my coffee to my assistants. No one dares cross me. I can't imagine allowing anyone to do anything hurtful to me." Vem, Cedar and Cosmo would make easy victims for someone like me. I am just as manipulative as my mother.

I look over at Vem and realize she has been staring at me, wide-eyed. I squeeze her hand. "You did the right thing."

"You were in your own cult then?" Vem asks, releasing my hand.

I shrug, sheepishly. "Nothing like yours. I could wear real clothes and..."

"You asked me about my relationship with Cedar the other day. I feel like I owe you an explanation of that history." She starts walking fast but then seeing how I'm not about to speed up to meet her, she slows down. "Cedar was Zion's favorite. He called her 'Dear Cedar'. Ugh. All the kids were allowed to do adult jobs if they wanted, so he chose her to be his assistant."

She pauses, wiping her nose on the sleeve of her coat. I'm glad it's the other hand she's using, just in case she needs another bout of touching on the way down. "There wasn't much parenting going on, what with all the classes our parents were taking on how to be a good human. Isn't that ironic?" She honks like a duck. Still haven't gotten used to that sound.

"When we weren't in school, we could learn to account, do food preparation, and all sorts of things that turned out to be very useful in life. I'll give Zion credit for that one." She licks a finger and sticks it in the air, as if adding a plus to his barren account. "Well, I should clarify, we could learn the things we wanted if there was space for us. But the things that were the most popular, like learning how to bake something magnificent or designing whatever ridiculous outfit the whole group would wear next, those jobs went by seniority. And you only moved up in seniority if you gave up your play time to do grunt work for Zion. Giving him shoulder rubs, clean his sleeping area; those kinds of things."

My eyes widen. "Oh, no!"

"No, it's not what you're thinking. He just made you do things a grown up shouldn't ask, like scrubbing his feet and ironing his sheets before he got into bed. Cedar didn't seem to have any problems doing things like that. Since her parents abandoned them for their own duties, she had lots of free time."

"And yours didn't?"

Vem hums in a low tone. This is a new display for her. I stop and stare.

"What are you doing?"

I pull out my phone and check my timer. Only seven minutes have gone by.

"I had to center my mind before replying. I don't want to become angry about things that are history. At Fallen Branch, men had to dye their hair gray and wear short beards, just like him. Women had short dark, bobs so they wouldn't stand out. We all wore the same color clothing every day. When the color changed, we all changed. It was hard to pick your parents out of the adults as they passed by you in the camp. They all looked the same and gave that same vacant smile. 'Hello young mind,' they would say as you passed. As a child you start to assume they're all your parents. It really messes with your head." She takes in a long, deep breath and lets it out slowly. "My parents did come visit me, in the middle of the night. I wasn't quite sure who they were. That's the part that's so hard to swallow."

She begins to hum again and I decide to keep walking. I yell over my shoulder, hoping she'll be motivated to move to hear me. "Cedar decided to do the accounting for the group?"

She walks quickly and is soon by my side. "It was something lots of kids wanted to learn. Who doesn't want to be in charge of spending money? 'Dear Cedar deserves to learn money. Dear Cedar will bring continued prosperity to our community.' Some days, I really hated her."

I pause to take a breath after we've climbed yesterday's challenging section, but find I'm not as out-of-breath as I was twenty-four hours ago.

"I think I can keep going!" I announce triumphantly. Vem nods and continues on.

"Zion's plan was to take over the town of Flanagan. That's what it was called then, and he hated that name. He said the sisters were an abomination, and he wanted to change the name to Fallen Branch, like the commune. If we all worked together, the commune and the town, we could make it a big industrial center. They would manufacture Zion Wear outdoor clothing on the site of the former Scheddy Salmon Cannery and have people from Fallen Branch work there. 'Revive the economy' was what he said. He thought they could make this a town full of industry. Instead, we're a tourist destination. Well, not really a destination, more like a stop-for-coffee-on-your-way-to-somewhere-else place."

"His plan actually sounds good. I mean, you want those things, right?"

"It would be fine and cherry pie, except that he didn't want anyone here who wasn't a member of Fallen Branch. He wanted everyone wearing the same community clothing, eating the same things and never inviting outsiders, to keep costs down. The only income from the city would come from manufacturing and fruits they harvested. They would ship things all over the world. He wanted to keep people with new ideas out, so he was the only one in charge of everyone's minds."

"Zion sounds like quite a politician."

Vem stops and stares me down. Second time this morning. "Not a politician. A dangerous man. Really dangerous. Those brown eyes of his were hollow-point bullets. When he stared at you, a part of you died."

I daydream about Cosmo's crystal blue eyes. A girl could get lost in those. *Stop it.*

"The night of the city council meeting, he brought a slide show and statistics, all acquired by Cedar, of course. We were best friends then. I helped her for months, when we were allowed to be together." She stares at the falls, or maybe she's in a meditative trance. I'm learning not to ask.

"It was a packed house," Vem continues. "Everyone who lived here wanted to make sure they weren't going to wake up tomorrow in a nightmare. The other side of the room was nothing but spacey-eyed people in olive green pajamas. I think it was olive green that year.

"After Cedar gave her entire speech, trying to convince everyone this would be the best thing for Flanagan and this cult really wasn't going to shove out the townies, our side of the room stood up and clapped, just like they were trained to do. The other folks, well they saw the big flaws in the plan.

"When she sat down, Zion put one beefy hand in the air. The man had the largest hands I've ever seen. I still think about them to this—"

"What did he say?" I interrupt. I think about the marketing opportunities, starting from scratch with a town.

"I don't know for sure. I couldn't understand. I was standing in the back and we were told to leave at a specific time, so everyone just got up and started filing out. I waited for a bit, wanting to talk to Cedar. When she finally left, she pushed me away and just ran."

"That's it?"

"Well, while I was standing where I wasn't supposed to be standing, I heard Zion telling someone he had a better plan. They would understand better in the morning. Zion's plan was never to be questioned. That's when I started walking back to Fallen Branch."

Vem stops and pulls my arm. She points to something in the distance. "We're almost there. Little Cone. It wasn't so hard, was it?"

I look ahead to a short waterfall that gently stair-steps its way into Aisley River. The sound of the water sliding down the rock steps is peaceful and calming. I already feel better.

"That's when Cosmo...killed him?" It's hard to spit those words out. He doesn't seem like the kind of person who would do that, even in an extreme fit of rage.

We continue on a few hundred feet, where we are standing next to a wooden fence and a viewing platform. There is a bench where I plop, not caring if Vem judges me.

She sits down next to me and takes in a deep breath, her hands rising with her chest. She lets it out slowly, bringing her hands back to waist level and then turns toward me. "It's still hard for me some days to think about. Cos just adored his sister. He followed her around like a little puppy. She was always driven, always wanting something more. His goal in life was just to be by her side. Lovely, if it weren't so tragic." She takes in another deep breath, following the same pattern. I do the same, realizing how good it feels.

"The story goes that he followed her out of the building," she continues. "Cedar was screaming that she would make Zion pay for humiliating her. I never witnessed it, but that's what everyone else said. She would reveal his secrets, ruin him, all the things you would expect. Cosmo went after her but she yelled at him to leave her alone. Cedar was furious. Poor Cosmo felt shoved aside."

I'm trying to picture Cedar, the most composed person I've met in this town so far, being that out of control. The thought of Cosmo standing dejected with no one else who cared makes my heart hurt. "They were just teens, right?"

Vem nods. "The next day, we all heard Cosmo killed Zion. I kind of thought it would be Cedar who came to a violent end, after the way she screamed and carried on."

I take in a deep breath, just as Vem has done and let it out slowly, without the added sounds. "Maybe I'm writing the wrong story."

Dearest Da,

You taught us to weather our burdens with the strength of a hundred men. Sometimes they become too much though, for even our broad shoulders to carry. It is still hard for me to think about this horror, but I must relay this next chapter of our lives in America.

With the canning season done for this year, Charles and Alfred Todd felt another adventure in order. We have four men from the cannery who help with the extra work in the off season. Mr. Samuel Li's brother, Jonas as he likes to be called, takes charge of planting and harvesting. The bairns have come to love his stories of China and he has taught them some of his language.

Over at Sister Faye's, Lachlan Douglas, an Irishman with jolly green eyes and a permanent chuckle on his face, oversees the daily operations. He's always got a bairn, mine or Faye's, by his side. While Mr. Samuel Li teaches geography and math, Lachlan Douglas educates the children in the running of a farm. They clean barns, pull weeds and milk cows under his watchful eye.

I'd recently noticed the light returning to Sister Faye's eyes. She enjoys Lachlan Douglas as much as her wee ones, and happily chatters to him like an old confidant. When he leaves for the day, she is back to her vacant self. Lachlan Douglas stayed for a hearty supper at her place on more than one occasion. I suppose I should voice my disapproval for this situation, but I cannot. Sister Faye re-emerging from the darkness is somewhat miraculous. If the company of Lachlan Douglas is what it takes, then I'll not let my prudish thoughts get in the way.

I received joyful letters from Charles, sent from all over the country regaling us with tales of life in the still-untamed parts of America. This trip took them to the Dakotas. The natives, once a mighty people who ruled the prairies with fierce pride, are now caged on lands that for us would be spacious. For these mighty hunters and nomads, it must seem like they are in small prison cells.

Charles, possessing the fever to roam himself, had a particular heartache seeing the way they were forced to wear our clothing and learn our language. He promised the children he would bring back skins from his bison hunt. They were guided by a very sad native who told them his people weren't allowed to hunt this particular area because the tourists, like Charles and Alfred Todd were to have the prime choice of animals.

That letter came two months ago, and I hadn't received another letter from Charles, but handing my worry to Mr. Samuel Li, I didn't concern myself with his absence. I knew he would return before canning season began. I've known him to become so involved in his daily activities he forgets for a time about his family. I don't mind. We are quite engrossed in our own lives here.

As you can see, Da, life appeared almost idyllic. We all felt gratitude for Sister Faye's changed behavior. Had I kept my suspicious nature closer at hand, I would not have been brought to my knees by what happened next.

I was out inspecting the harvest of potatoes, beans, corn, and onions (for our use as well as the employees who have families and don't make enough to feed them) as I always do. I made sure all were well supplied with lemonade flavored with lavender needles when a strange man and woman strode slowly up our lane. It's not an easy climb, though the reward of flat ground and a view of the ocean is enough to make it.

Their somber faces told me more than I wanted to know. The man, carrying a Bible and a handkerchief, introduced himself as a minister residing in Astoria, Oregon. His wife was accompanying him. They were here to bring the grim news of the recovery of three bodies on their shores last week.

The first, that of my beloved Charles, was said to

be well dressed and had no visible wounds. In his breast pocket was a smeared drawing that I recognized as Sarah's family picture she had so lovingly included in our last correspondence with him. At the time, I thought him to be in Kansas City.

The second body was that of a woman, well dressed, in her early twenties. She was missing part of her hand and both of her shoes. The third, and Da, the most shocking was the condition of Alfred Todd. You see, he was also well-dressed, freshly shaven, and carrying in his breast pocket a marriage license confirming his union to a Miss Daisy Congruse.

The minister carried the document with him, for he must've known I would be skeptical of this wild story. Sure enough, I saw the name of my brother-in-law and his signature at the bottom. In the "witness" box was none other than my Charles. My principled husband took part in this farce?

I must've gasped while reading, because the minister's wife took my arm and asked if I would like to sit. Realizing there was nowhere but bare ground, I politely declined. The minister offered the handkerchief. There was more to this story, he added grimly. When they washed up on shore Alfred Todd had a bullet hole in his skull; Charles and the woman likely drowned.

I could barely breathe. This was too much for me, and as it was sinking in, I wondered how poor Sister Faye might handle it. She had just recently lost her delicate countenance. I didn't want to share with her the details of her husband's death and swore the minister and his wife to secrecy.

The bodies would be coming in three days' time, so I would have to bring the news of Alfred Todd's demise to Sister Faye sooner than I wanted. I couldn't tell her the entire story just yet. The kind couple offered to stay and help me tell the family, but I didn't need help destroying their lives.

"And what of this Daisy?" I asked. "What will become of her?" I wasn't sure why I cared. The minister stared at the ground as he explained she resided in a house of ill repute before her betrothal, and the madam assured him they would contact her family as soon as they could.

I needed to see for myself this body they were bringing was in fact my beloved Charles. I asked if I could go to the morgue by myself before informing Sister Faye of this unfathomable event. The minister looked at me with horror. "Oh no," I assured him, "I've seen a man in final repose before. I won't become faint."

He shook his head and pointed behind me, where my dear Sarah was standing, hands over her tiny mouth and eyes full of tears. She ran to me and held me tight. "I'll go with you, Mam," she said bravely.

I tried to resist, but there was nothing I could do to keep her from accompanying me. That's our courageous, strang girl. None of the events in our hard life by the sea has caused her to shy from it.

The next day, while Sister Faye happily and unsuspectingly watched my boys, Sarah and I found our way to the building between the general store and the biggest bar in town, Millie's Saloon. We held each other tightly as we were guided into a cold room, heavy with the smell of death.

They pulled back the sheet to reveal Charles' pure face, grey in color. His lips were parted as if trying to say my name in his last gasp for air. I looked to my darling dochter, worried for what might happen seeing her faither in such a state.

Sarah reached down to touch his face, fascinated by its waxen appearance. "No, miss." The stern man slapped her hand away. "That's not allowed."

She is of sturdy, Flanagan stock, Da. I've known that since she pulled her cousin, Padrug from the sea as a wave was about to crash on his little head. Sister Faye would have been without another bairn, too much loss for anyone, let alone our frail Sister Faye. A twelve-year-old with more presence than many a grown woman.

Sarah grasped my hand tightly. "He looks at peace, Mam. I doubt he suffered. Shall we see Uncle now?"

I nodded my head reluctantly. Quite fittingly, my brother-in-law was missing a portion of his mouth. Eaten by a sea creature, no doubt. Sarah didn't blink at that either.

"Did Uncle die from the bullet, or did he drown first?" she asked, almost too eagerly.

The coroner explained Charles and Daisy had water in their lungs, but Albert Todd did not. My darling husband and that horrid woman drowned, while Albert Todd was the victim of a gunshot.

Sarah looked to me for explanation but I had none. I promised her we would find the answers. First, though, we had to accomplish an equally difficult task: putting one more crack in Sister Faye's heart.

Your Devoted Dochter,
Fiona Flanagan Scheddy

Chapter Seventeen

PINEY FALLS, OREGON

I've put it off long enough. As I'm walking up the steps, I wonder what I'm going to say. We're not friends. In the business world, politeness is usually enough to get the information you want. In Piney Falls, it takes some kind of magic I haven't discovered yet.

"Hi Cedar! Remember me from the other day?" I stick out my hand. She hesitates before accepting my gesture. Today she is wearing a turquoise blouse with a black-and-white sweater over the top, and dangling grey earrings. They make her eyes sharp and clear. It's too bad she and Vem aren't speaking, she could offer some useful fashion tips.

"Yeah, I remember. I don't have anything else to tell you, sorry." She pushes her silver hair behind her ear and looks down at the same papers she gave to me the last time I came in. She has been doodling on them, drawing detailed faces. Some are cherubic, others are evil, with pointed chins.

"I'm staying out on Magnificent Drive. My neighbor is November Bean. She said you two were friends long ago."

She looks up and her unfriendly face turns to ice. "Yes, I know who she is."

"She was telling me you might have information on the cult...commune, that used to be in operation outside of town. I'm thinking of changing the focus of my research a little."

She stares at me for a minute and then walks into the back room. I'm not sure if I should continue to stand there. Maybe she's gone to get a weapon. Maybe she left out the back door. I try to imagine this building when it was brand new - the Flanagan sisters parading around in all of their finery, telling people what to do. Many years later, all of the Fallen Branch members just as much the new members of society, standing in the lobby waiting for instructions on how to start a new life.

"These are all the handouts we printed on Fallen Branch." She hands me one piece of paper that gives me basic information. Four paragraphs, tops. There is an overly complicated design on the top, swirling lines intersecting with intricate designs in each space.

"I didn't want a handout. I wanted you to tell me about it."

"Why?"

"Because it's a part of this town's history. Maybe

there's something you can remember to help me. The Flanagan sisters, maybe they're just part of this story." I smile broadly.

"Nothing is connected!" she snaps. "I don't know why you have to drag all of this up. We've put Fallen Branch behind us."

"Maybe you haven't. If nobody can talk about it, then you're all still struggling with whatever happened." I lean across the counter, something I learned to do in Mark Brawley's Reaching Out to Meet Your Client Seminar. *If they are timid, physically draw them in.* She takes a step back.

"I grew up watching my parents from a distance. When I scraped my knee or had a bad day, they didn't care. Half the time they didn't even remember they had children. It's not something I want to talk about. Nobody else in this town does, either."

"But if you did... Please? It's just a silly story, and..."

She sighs. "Your story may be silly. Mine isn't."

It hits me in the gut. I've never accepted "no" as an answer. The bottom line was always about results. Even when I didn't know what I was doing, I kept pushing for answers, no matter what the cost.

She doodles furiously. "One question. That's all you get."

"You and Vem..." I begin before wisely shutting my mouth. I have to think quickly.

"The night of the city council meeting, did you threaten to kill Zion?"

"Who have you been talking to?" She eyes me suspiciously.

"November Bean. She says you were good friends at one time. I mentioned that already."

Her face softens. "She was my buddy. When Cos was busy, she and I would sneak off and tell each other jokes. She kept me sane."

It's hard to think of Vem as the calming type; even with all of her exercises, she makes me anxious every time I see her. I don't know what sound or motion to expect next.

"There was peace in having a sense of order. Do this, get a reward. Do that, get a punishment. There were no surprises. Until the night of the city council meeting." She scratches her nose and turns away. "I was so proud of what I'd accomplished and the council laughed at me. It was humiliating. I knew Zion would come to my defense, though. He always protected me when the others were punished." She begins to sketch squares on her paper. Her hand is moving quickly, and the tip of her pencil breaks. "Instead, he stood up and talked about how I was just a kid who didn't comprehend his vision. He would make this place a model for the entire Oregon Coast. He'd do something completely different and the words coming out of my mouth were those of a lunatic. It was like he flipped a switch and became someone else. Out of nowhere, he decided all of my research was worthless. Just to please the townies."

"And then what?"

The color drains from her face. "What do you mean?"

"I mean, what happened next? I know that he was found dead the next day."

She pulls her sweater off the back of her chair and wraps it around her shoulders. "I told you I would answer one question."

"I have a...contract...to write a story." I've never told a lie that didn't have a purpose. "I could write about the Flanagan sisters, or I could write about Fallen Branch and the secrets that are still here."

"Lanie, Miss Anders, this is all over. There's no need to drag it back to the sur—"

"It's not over. This town is asleep. No one wants to do anything to move it forward. Your marketing strategy to sell tourism is one crazy cop with a speech, and some strange nametags. People are dying at those falls. I don't believe they're all just jumping because it's the thing to do. Wouldn't it be amazing if you could be the great leader Zion never was? Take control and show everyone how to get these secrets out into the daylight so they can't harm people anymore?"

She folds her arms tightly across her chest. "I never saw him. I left in tears that night and ran all the way back to the commune by myself. People gossiped that I threatened him. I didn't. Even though I knew things..."

She pauses to suck in a big gulp of air. "All the way home, I was thinking of ways I could really get back at him, like standing up during our group time and telling everyone how we were being financed. We weren't self-sufficient like he told everyone.'

"When I heard what Cosmo did, I knew he was just defending my honor. I loved him so much for that. But it hurt too much, and I didn't want to hear what my sweet, sweet Cosmo felt forced to do for me. I didn't need the picture of my brother killing someone in my head. Especially someone with secrets he needed to hear."

Chapter Eighteen

Dearest Da,

I've spent more than three months trying to put together Charles' last minutes of life. He must've found himself in an intolerable situation with Alfred Todd's polygamy. Conflicted about his role. Should he be the older brother, supportive, or should he be concerned with his position as faithful husband and faither?

He always took his pistol on their trips in case they encountered unsavory types. Maybe when they were finally out at sea, he could take it no more and shot his brother, just as a giant wave overtook them. I shall remember my husband as brave and noble.

You would assume after suffering so much loss that Sister Faye would be bereft and unable to care for herself. You might also assume the child she was carrying, the last tangible connection between a husband

and wife would become a source of pain and darkness for our dear Sister Faye.

After I told her that Alfred Todd had been swept out to sea, I added that he had been on an adventure looking for an octopus, one of his lifelong fascinations. Though that seemed to satisfy her grieving heart, her bairns had more questions. "Why was Da adventuring so close by? Why didn't he take us with him?"

I can't even remember what I told them, Da, myself still being in a fog of grief. I wanted their questions to end so I could take care of my own broken soul.

I convinced Sister Faye she must not view the body of her beloved Alfred Todd. The sea can be harsh to those it claims, I reminded her.

Mrs. Aisley made her cinnamon berry cake and each of the foremen stood up to tell a good story about their bosses. Lachlan Douglas remembered the time Alfred Todd gave him the afternoon to bury one of the many drowned sailors that washed up on the beach. Lachlan Douglas found the man to be of Irish descent, like himself and wanted him to have a proper burial. As is the custom, those with unknown origins are buried where they came to shore.

Lachlan Douglas didn't realize that after the tide goes out, if buried shallow, the bodies will re-appear. To his horror, on his way home from work he heard a young girl screaming for her mam that a man came up from the depths of hell to punish her for not finishing her fish-head stew.

Although tired and recovering from an ailment in his chest, Charles, and later Alfred Todd, brought shovels and began to help dig a proper grave for the man. It was dark before they finished and gave the man a decent service, thanking him for his devotion to his ship and his job before covering him with enough earth to prevent further terrors for small bairns.

I noticed as soon as the service for our husbands ended that Sister Faye and Lachlan Douglas were laughing and talking out by the barn, away from those who came to pay their respects. I wanted to admonish Sister Faye for disrespecting her husband in such a public and shameful way. There was something that seemed quite joyous in her manner, and knowing what she had been through in the previous years, I dared not interrupt her in a brief moment of happiness.

The children took their cue from their mother, seeing it was alright to enjoy the sun and breathe in the fine smell of pine trees. They ran and frolicked for the love of all that is life and living. Mine did the same, and by the end of the day, their cheeks were flushed and they slept well. I remembered them doing the same a hundred times while their faithers sipped whiskey on the porch. I knew the next day they would wake up with feelings of sorrow once more.

Several men voiced concern about the future of the cannery. I assured them Scheddy Salmon Cannery would continue. After all, it had been Sister Faye and myself doing the bookwark, reporting mechanical issues and tending to little details during the day. Our husbands, fun-loving happy men devoted to family (at least I thought) and homestead, were not good at running a business.

While helping clean the dishes and tidy the kitchen, Mrs. Aisley whispered that her husband intended to offer us a fair price for the cannery soon. I was shocked. He knew nothing of our business and we nothing of his. Why would he need a cannery?

I remarked that Sister Faye and I were planning to continue to run the business by ourselves. "What?" She chuckled loudly. "Two women can't run a cannery. It isn't done. Take your children to California with me and they shall grow up with a good education. Your dochter will marry well and your sons will start their own businesses."

I smiled and nodded, knowing Sister Faye and I would need to further discuss issues before announcing our formal plans.

By the time Mr. Stanford Aisley visited our home, Sister Faye and I were already firm to keep Scheddy Salmon Cannery in business. When we informed him of our wishes, he not only laughed heartily like his wife, but also exclaimed, "Once I tell your husbands' customers you aren't qualified to run the business nor to keep equipment repaired, they'll leave quite quickly. There are plenty of canneries on the coast run by good men. They need not be burdened with the likes of two hapless widows."

Sister Faye clasped her hands in her lap, as she always did when Alfred Todd was lecturing her on a topic of which she possessed twice the knowledge. She waited patiently for him to finish before taking a deep breath. "Mr. Stanford Aisley, we sisters shaa continue in th' manner we hae fur th' pest twal years. We'll help label th' cans an' plan monthly dinners fur uir warkmen oan Friday evenings. Th' operation will be under th' charge of Mr. Lachlan Douglas."

He eyed us doubtfully, but the more Sister Faye spoke, the more he seemed agreeable to our plan. After receiving our assurance that Lachlan Douglas was well qualified for the job, having been in our employ, or rather our husbands' employ for seven years, he left, satisfied things would be under the capable eye of a male.

Well Da, behind the curtain, we made our deal with Lachlan Douglas. You'd call it a deal wi' th' devil himself. Lachlan Douglas would oversee operations as Sister Faye and I continued to do the books, running our inspections of equipment and thorough cleaning. Lachlan Douglas would be the face of our company only, for a nice increase in pay. He, being sweet on Sister Faye, readily agreed to our terms. What man wouldn't want a title that required little in the way of labor to achieve?

It was at least three weeks later when I finally had the strength to go back to the cannery. To my horror, a large hole had been cut from the floor. Lachlan Douglas explained he caught one of the employees trying to steal whatever money Albert Todd kept in his private safe. I checked the desk drawer for the *sgian-*

dubh. It was still there, where Charles and I placed it years ago.

It was news to me that Albert Todd had a private safe. Lachlan Douglas showed me a heavy, metal box that had been forced open. Inside was the necklace he bought Sister Faye for Christmas last year. Nothing else remained.

Lachlan Douglas promised to track down the thief and make sure he was brought to justice. In our community, that meant being forced into servitude aboard a large commercial vessel or spending weeks in the city jail. The police don't always come to work, sometimes too drunk to care. Those who are incarcerated often go days without food or water until someone cares to check on them. I asked him to instead give the criminal a job cleaning floors.

He agreed, but somehow, I doubted he believed in my form of justice.

Your Devoted Dochter,

Fiona Flanagan Scheddy

Chapter Nineteen

PINEY FALLS, OREGON

As I head off into the woods, on the pathway Vem said wasn't used any more, I realize there is something unfamiliar in my gut: guilt, like the kind I felt for taking advantage of Carl Jackson.

Whatever wound has opened for me here just won't close. It's not just Carl, it's Steven and Malcom and Ted... The list is endless. I didn't know them or care to. I just wanted to use them for a few hours. Lanie Anders, one of the best marketing consultants in the country is also a world class jerk. That hits me with a thud.

I sit down on a tree stump with a pen and paper, pushing these new feelings aside so I can write something. A story of a vain man who forced his will on a group of people too eager to please. *He is just like me.* It's not interesting at all. I try for a few more minutes to compose a fictional account of Fiona and Faye

Scheddy's life. They were remarkable women who deserve much more than a silly attempt at a pretend story of their life.

Vem taught me to open my arms to the sky and invite the information from the universe. It's worth a try. I open my arms like a bird and thrust my head back, wiling something creative to enter my brain. My neck starts to hurt and I lower my arms and bend my head toward the ground, where I see something shiny. A round, silver medallion. I pick it up and notice the object is polished and bright, probably dropped out here just recently. There is writing on one side, *Grand Plan 1984.* I turn it over to discover a farm scene, one of rolling hills and a single stalk of some plant in the front.

I look around. There is no one else here. This pathway is definitely still in use, no matter what Vem says. I stick the medallion in my pocket and walk back.

When I get close to my rental, I see Vem waiting on my porch. She jumps up excitedly, like she has springs on her feet when I approach.

"Where have you been, neighbor friend? I've been looking all over for you. I have news about your search! I decided to help my brother's wife, Peony, year of the P, go through his things. I found this in the attic, hidden away. It was written by Fiona Scheddy to the hospital before she and her sister jumped over the falls."

Unable to focus on anything else, I thrust the medal in her face. "What's this?" I ask.

Her face drops. "No... Where did you find that?"

"In the forest. On the ground. Who does this belong to?"

She folds her arms and turns to view the ocean. "We all had to wear identification medals. All designed according to your letter year and completely vanilla. All were pretty boring, except this one. It was Zion's. He wore it all the time. There's a farm scene on the back, like he thought he was creating this whole new universe for us." She turns so her back is completely facing me.

"I decided to make my own, something that would represent me and not just the people who were born in the year of the N. That was my little bit of defiance. Also, I made them for my friends, each one a little different. My workmate, Carlton, Year of the C, was so excited, he found his father and showed it to him. His father, being a loyal Fallen Branch member, took the medallion and turned in his son for wearing something that wasn't Fallen Branch compliant. We were all supposed to destroy them, but I refused."

She seems lost in a deep memory and I don't want to disturb her.

"I told Carlton maybe his father wanted to keep it as a memento. Carlton treasured that memory, even though we both knew it wasn't possible. Isn't that silly?"

"Not silly at all." I pat her back. "And what about Zion's medallion?"

"When they pulled him out of the water, he was so

disfigured they decided his medallion was lost in the struggle."

I shudder, thinking of sweet, kind, Cosmo. I still can't wrap my mind around him committing such a violent act. It seems out of character for such a kind man. An incredibly handsome, kind man. "It somehow ended up in the forest a mile from the falls? That seems odd."

"Actually," Vem clears her throat. "I found it. When I first moved back here. I was out walking and there it was, sitting in the middle of a shrine someone had created. There were all sorts of artifacts from Fallen Branch. I decided that was the worst symbol of our lives in the commune. I performed a purification ceremony and moved it to another area. Letting nature re-take it." She spins back around, evidently cleansed of her bad thoughts.

I study her face for any signs of dishonesty. It's a peculiar thing not to mention on our many walks. "Is there more to this story?"

"Always. With Fallen Branch, you never reach the end." She replies simply. "Do you want to see this letter or not?"

"Of course I do. Thank you so much for sharing it with me."

Dear Staff of Flanagan City Hospital,

After the loss of our sweet boy, Wee Hiram, we found it so difficult to go on with our lives. His death came not because we weren't by his side, but because help was too far away. He would have grown into a fine caring man.

Knowing how much he loved the animals in the woods and his own cousin, he would have been so pleased to know this hospital was started in his honor. Dear Fiona and I wanted to ensure no other child would lose their life because help was too far away.

We decided to find the best doctors in the country to staff our hospital. We were the first in the area to allow people of all nationalities to enter whether they were able to pay or not. Being strong, immigrant women, we marvel at all that is possible for us in this country. That's why we made sure to hire women doctors. They'll be more plentiful in the future, of that we are most certain.

Our Sarah eagerly awaits her education in the medical field. We ask that in the name of this strang girl, you continue to search the country for good women to complete your staff.

With all my appreciation,

Faye Flanagan, as told to Fiona Flanagan

"Vem, where did you get this letter?"

She clears her throat again. "My brother. The mayor. Former."

I gasp. "Mayor Britain is...was...your brother?

"Nochturn. Born in the year of the N. Some of us changed our names after Fallen Branch ended." There is no change in her demeanor.

"I'm so sorry for your loss! Oh Vem, it must be so painful! You never mentioned..."

Vem looks at her large-faced watch. "I have to go. Incense burning at noon. We'll hike tomorrow."

I nod. I shouldn't be surprised she has trouble with

emotion, with the life she's led. There is research to be done, so I can't spend my day studying Vem.

I decide to search public records, a building across the street from Cedar's office. The woman who unlocks the door to let me in looks like she's fast approaching 100. I don't think I'm supposed to have access to everything in this room, but I'm not going to point that out. I'm also not going to ask if these things are available online. I doubt she's ever tried using a computer, let alone the Internet.

"Do you have any information on the Scheddy family? Maybe a deed of sale for the land?"

Welcome to Piney Falls! Hi, I'm Gladys. Ask me about our 2 beach umbrellas for rent. She pinches her face. "Why would you want that?"

"For research purposes. Historical. That's all." She stares at me for a few moments, eyeing me up and down.

Abruptly, she shuffles slowly to another room and returns after an incredibly lengthy absence. She flops a piece of paper on the counter. "Here ya go, miss. The land was owned by the Fallen Branch nuts. Ever since that fell apart, it's been sitting there without any inter-est. You thinkin' of buying it? Kids go there to drink and probably fornicate. You really want that headache?"

I ignore her comments. "What would Fallen Branch want with the Flanagan property? Were they going to expand?"

Gladys folds her arms across her ample chest.

"Imagine they had all sorts of plans, none of them good. Human sacrifice, devil worshippin' and the like. Those are the floaters now, you know. Who can blame them, what with the way they carried on?"

For some reason, she's gotten under my skin. "Many of us have done things we're not exactly proud of. That's not a reason to jump off the falls. It's been long enough. This town needs to accept these poor people and let them get on with their lives!" My voice has risen to a point it is echoing in this spacious building.

I take the paper and leave, without saying more. It's not the Fallen Branch members I'm talking about. It's me.

Chapter Twenty

AISLEY LUMBER TOWNSHIP, OREGON

Dearest Da,

That day we met, Charles and Albert Todd were coming out of the pub, laughing. "Now there's some jolly American wee jimmies," you remarked. Charles asked you for directions and instead, you invited them both to dinner. We'd never seen you quite so forward, at least not as far back as I could remember. After Mam died, even neighbors hadn't been welcomed in our home.

Sister Faye and I, not having experience entertaining, worked furiously to impress our American guests. The scotch broth we'd been saving to fight the winter cough, our special recipe haggis, oatcakes, and whisky filled the table.

Sister Faye later confessed she hoped our meal might impress these boys enough to offer to take our own strang brothers to carry their luggage on their travels. Instead, Alfred Todd couldn't take his eyes off sweet Faye. She hadn't any experience with men outside the family and refused to meet his gaze.

They asked to see us again the next night, but we had little time or money to acquire more food to entertain. Charles asked if he might walk with me in the moonlight. Just like Sister Faye, I'd had no experience to know what might be appropriate behavior for a young lass.

He asked polite questions and I blathered about my life as if I'd never been given the gift of speech before. I told him of Mam's origins in New York, words we weren't allowed to remember in front of you. I mentioned her premonition of her bairn returning to her homeland.

Charles nodded sympathetically. At one point, on that very first night, he took my hand and kissed it. "My heart aches for you, Dear Fiona," he said. I only confess his behavior now that an ocean separates us from your rage over his inappropriate action.

I confessed we wouldn't be able to make another feast for them, but Sister Faye and I would very much like to see them again. In truth, I had no idea if Sister Faye liked Alfred Todd, just that she acted silly in his presence.

That next morning, when Neighbor Campbell showed up with his wagon piled high with goods, our eyes were bright and our stomachs moving with anticipation of the meals would we have.

"Whaur did thes come frae?" You asked, suspicious

of the neighbor who told you to sell your bairn lest they turn out like their Mam.

"From the Americans in town."

That was all it took to win Faye's heart. In truth, mine was already given to Charles Scheddy. Faye and I were so eager to join them on their journey, wherever it might take us. After listening to Mam talk of America, it seemed like destiny we would marry them and have a good life together. After a month's time, they were to leave. You didn't have a problem giving your lass' hands in marriage to two jolly strangers. I tell you now that I have a good idea why.

Charles confided shortly into our stay in New York that he spoke with you in the barn the day before asking to make me his wife. He promised he would care for me always. He could tell you weren't convinced we should both go.

That's when he told you I confessed everything. In my excitement over seeing a new face outside the family, I acted out our story, right there in the barn. I showed him where you were, where Mam was. Ten years on, those demons needed to come out, Da.

He paid you a tidy sum for the hands of your dochters and pledged he would never mention what happened to anyone. I can't imagine your face during such a transaction. Did it sadden you? Did you feel relief?

Now when I go up the hill to visit him, I ask why he didn't think I was worth more than an assurance of his silence. I've always been sure of his love. It's just now that he's passed that I wonder why Fiona Flanagan couldn't be special enough for both of you without all of that. I don't mean to be insolent. Being alone can do things to the mind, letting it go where it might not otherwise.

As I sat beside his grave yesterday, I was approached by Lachlan Douglas. He didn't worry himself with a widow in intimate thought beside her husband's buried body.

"Mrs. Scheddy, this is of utmost importance," he said, the jolliness he displayed around Faye completely absent.

He admitted he had been speaking with Mr. Stanford Aisley about uses for the building in the off-season. He had great plans to combine our building with the needs of Aisley Lumber Mill. "It's all been settled. In my position as manager, I'm able to make these decisions without your knowledge. I thought it the gentlemanly thing to do to inform you."

I was stunned, though I shouldn't have been. Later, Mr. Samuel Li came to our door. "Watch him as closely as you can, please," I begged.

He nodded. "Don't worry, Mrs. Scheddy. The person who tries to travel two roads gets nowhere."

That's all for now.

Your Devoted Dochter,

Fiona Flanagan Scheddy

Chapter Twenty-One

PINEY FALLS, OREGON

"Thanks so much for keeping an eye on things, Dancinee."

"Mmmhm." She's not doing a great job of hiding her annoyance with me. I tried to explain to her during my time on her couch that we have to give off the vibe we're interested at all times, even when we're not. That's how you succeed in the business world.

"Did I tell you about Cosmo? He's a strange but lovely man. Everyone here is a little off, as a matter of fact. But it's been good for me. Even though I'm eating pastries on a regular basis, I've lost four pounds and my whole perspective on life has changed."

She is silent.

"So," I continue, "the other day I was hiking Little Cone Falls and it struck me: the reason I never reached out to my 'rich friends' as you called them. They were business acquaintances, that's all. Friends of convenience. My neighbor, Vem coined that term."

"Man. You're just…you still don't see the big picture."

What does she know of the big picture? I keep my mouth closed.

"I let you stay with me, even though I didn't have the room. I even let you re-arrange my cereal. But it's time you got real with yourself. You are a lady who has to control everything in your life. Your friends, your house, even people like me you don't really know. You gave everyone MY number, like I'm your personal assistant because you don't know how to have a regular relationship with humans. Firing people because they looked at you wrong. You're going to crush this poor space guy…"

"Cosmo." It pops out of my mouth before I can stop myself.

"He's the perfect mark for you because he doesn't know enough to understand you're going to steam roll over him and leave him in the gutter too. You'll sleep with him and throw him away."

It hits me hard. Am I really that awful? Did all of those men really expect more from me? "That's a horrible thing to say. That I'm only interested in him because of his tragic background. Really out of line, Dancinee."

"Is it? Tell you what: the next time you think about calling me, ask yourself first, 'Did I sleep with this space guy and throw him away?' If so, don't call me back. I'll be mad that I'm right," she huffs. "And that architect guy? He hit on me. He's, like, my mom's age."

"I'm sorry, Dancinee. I'll compensate you for your—"

"Do you even want to build this house? Live here? In the three times you've called and all the lengthy voicemail messages, you've never mentioned either one. For all that you claim to know, you are pretty clueless when it comes to life stuff, Lanie. Once you get back, I don't want to deal with these people any more. You've got to take care of your own problems. I'm already late for work. Some of us need jobs, remember?"

I want to crawl under my bed. I've never felt so humiliated. For a moment I revert to my old self: She's young and overworked. That's why she doesn't understand. But there is a new voice inside of me. I know she's right about everything.

"You're making sense. I should tell you—"

"No more confessions. I really need to leave soon or I'll miss my bus. Call your office, check in with your people and quit calling me, okay?"

There is another thud in my stomach. They've been coming so often; it could be the real reason I've lost weight. "I quit my job." It feels good to get that off my chest.

"You what?"

"The last day I was in town, I stopped by and told them I wasn't coming back. I was tired of living my life on the road, barely putting a dent in the Louis the Fourteenth sofa. I'll look for something else when I get back. I just couldn't figure out how to tell you."

"Then do yourself a favor and stay. There's nothing for you here."

Chapter Twenty-Two

AISLEY TOWNSHIP, OREGON

Dear Da,

It's been some time since our husband's bodies drifted in from sea. Sister Faye took the news of her husband's passing with the grace of a woman who had shooldered more than her share of burden in her twenty-nine years. She didn't crumble in tears the way she did when Wee Hiram died.

Instead, she began making sensible plans for her little family. First, she asked if she and the boys could move in with us. We have plenty of room in our house and in truth, the extra distraction is most welcome.

The dirt was barely over Charles and Alfred Todd (buried on either side of Wee Hiram) before she sat me down to tell me her next plan. She wished to turn her home into the first hospital in Aisley Lumber Township. She'd always felt the reason Wee Hiram passed was that we didn't have proper doctors here to care for him. I didn't have the heart to fight her on this.

Having someone to care for the sick might be a good thing.

"Makin' good out ay bad," she said.

"You're right, Faye. Making good out of bad, for our whole family. The bairn will learn more about caring for others than we could ever teach them," I told her.

Our workers agreed to convert the first floor into a waiting room with eight curtained areas. The second floor is the surgical area. Da, you wouldn't believe the surgeries that can be done. None that would have saved our Wee Hiram, but limbs no longer have to be severed from the body if mangled. They can be repaired. Bodies are opened and restored like some kind of magic. Faye hired surgeons from all over the country, each promising they would save a child such as Hiram with the advances in medicine since then. I don't believe they could. It was a powerful disease, but Faye does and that's all that matters. Faye assists as nurse when her time permits. She has taught Sarah basic care duties and it is hard to keep the lass away from the misery. The boys sweep floors and lift heavier patients.

As more and more in the community feel they can trust us and our new medicine, our road becomes quite busy. I don't know how you'll feel about this, but when we created the hospital, it was necessary to give the road a proper name. We called it Flanagan Lane.

I daresay this charitable deed became her obsession. She cared little for the well-being of Padrug and Percival unless they were helping patients in some way. It kept her mind from her troubles and Sarah didn't mind looking after the boys.

Faye decided to go back to her Flanagan name, for herself and her bairns, after the death of Albert Todd. Maybe she knows about his misdeeds somehow. I never told her. She forbids both Percival and Padrug from mentioning their Da lest their mouths be washed out with soap and reminded them they would never call themselves 'Scheddy' again.

Mrs. Aisley said I shouldn't worry myself with this disturbing behavior. The less the boys wallowed in the death of their faither, the quicker they would become strang young men.

For that reason, she's also named the hospital Flanagan Lane Hospital. She wanted to rename the cannery as well, but I told her that wouldn't be right, and if we were going to change the name that meant new labels on the cans. My bairn don't understand her need to erase their Scheddy heritage, but I told them to respect their auntie's decision to bring her old country to our new land. That seemed to be good enough.

Slowly, people began to trickle in. Sick children, men with injuries from the cannery, (there are many who sever fingers, I'm sad to report) and all kinds of ailments. They come from up and down the coast, some traveling a full days' drive to see our renown doctors. I'm proud of Faye's desire to help others.

Her third request shocked me the most, Da. It

came near six months after their deaths. By that time, she pretended like Alfred Todd never existed. I'm feeling such shame about what my fingers must write to you.

In my last letter I told you the story of Lachlan Douglas, our employee who agreed to act as manager of the cannery. We paid handsomely for him to act as a respectable man, someone who nods and agrees while the Flanagan sisters do the real work. At times, I've wondered if it was all so necessary. But then I see the working women in our community, four of them school marms, three nurses at the hospital and the others mostly in the business of prostitution. The place in this world for those of our persuasion, as Mam used to say, seems to be small and hidden in the dark.

Lachlan Douglas willingly helped us at first. He enjoyed his position, especially being able to boss around his friends and enemies. Sometimes we caught him making decisions without our knowledge or care. In one such an instance, he hired six new fishermen with their own boats. He paid them in advance for their catch. They never returned.

I should have known, Da. From the first day in our employ, when he grinned wide and inappropriate at Faye, he was a bad bodie. About four months in to our arrangement, he called me into the office. "Come to MY office, Mrs. Scheddy," he says. That was my first warning.

I closed to the door and informed him that he was indeed standing in an office, but that it was MY office and I'd thank him to remember that. He chuckled and pulled on his unkempt red beard.

He told me he called me in to tell me he was going to take control of more decisions, buying three new fishing boats for his cousins from Washington to use. "You'll not get a penny more than you're owed," I said firmly.

That made him chuckle once more. My blood was boiling, Da. "I'll remind you I'm doing you a favor," he says. "I can make things much worse for ya, Mrs. Scheddy. Things that would ruin your reputation as a respectable business woman."

He spills poison from his lips, smiling as he recounts Faye's visits to his room at all hours, like a common prostitute. The shock in my body right then, that Sister Faye would do such a thing. Then I remember I've been hearing noises at night that aren't the accustomed sounds of our home. In a large residence there are squeaks and squawks all night long. So many parts have to work in unison to keep the massive structure in place; it's a dance that we've grown accustomed to.

An ugliness seeps through my insides as I think about what could be the truth of this matter. Faye is lying to me. Lachlan Douglas has taken control of her heart and her mind. He has distracted her from family and her life's mission: the hospital. She would give up her dignity and place as a respected woman in the community for the company of a man who is nothing more than a snake oil salesman. He knows he has a hold on her, Sister Faye was alone so many years before her husband died and now, she will give all of her common sense to have someone by her side.

There was nothing I could do, if I wanted to preserve our places in this community. I sadly agreed to allow him to use our money for his unwise business decisions to save the reputation of Sister Faye. If only that were the end of the things.

I hadn't forgotten about the circumstances surrounding the death of Charles and Albert Todd. Under the guise of visiting a dress shop for Sarah, she and I left to visit Astoria, Oregon, up the coast where the bodies had been found. We brought Mr. Samuel Li along to act as our companion and protector. Astoria is known to be much wilder than Aisley Lumber Township.

Sarah, my twelve-year-auld lassie gonnae oan twin-tie, composed a list of questions for the coroner and others we found willing to disclose information. She even suggested we visit the madam who housed Albert Todd's paramour. I was shocked by her forwardness, but the more I thought of it, the more it seemed like the right thing to do. Oh, how Charles would have scolded me for allowing our dochter to visit such a place.

We stopped first at the coroner's office. He didn't want to speak to us about the details of their deaths. Mr. Samuel Li asked us to wait outside while he proceeded to persuade him otherwise. A few minutes later, both men came out to the porch, the coroner folding bills and placing them in his pocket.

He told us, with some reluctance, that he found Albert Todd had been inebriated and suspected there had been drinking involved before they entered the boat. Sarah scribbled furiously. He assured her that her own faither didn't smell of drink and was completely sober.

He showed us one of the photographs taken during the autopsy. He asked me twice if I felt it was appropriate for a young girl to view something so disturbing.

I suppressed a giggle. Aisley Lumber Township is full of violence and blood. Bodies wash on shore almost daily from the violent seas. Maybe the Aisley bairn are protected from the harshness of our world, but mine are not.

There, on Albert Todd's forehead near his hairline, was a distinct, square impression. It was in the shape of a broad tree, the Flanagan family crest. With a sick twist in my stomach, I realized my Charles must've punched his brother while wearing our beloved wedding gift from you.

"Did you find the ring then?" I asked, hopefully.

He shook his head no. "Many of the secrets of those who die at sea are lost to the violence of the ocean." He replied.

We continued on to the brothel, where once again Mr. Samuel Li went inside while Sarah and I stood at some distance. I didn't care so much for myself, but my dochter should become a lady without a bad reputation attached.

The woman in charge, a stern matron with dark hair and full lips, appeared on the porch. "I wish I could invite you in out of the chill," she pulled her shawl tightly around her broad shoolders.

I showed her the family pictures with Albert Todd and Charles standing proudly beside their bairn. She recognized them both, causing me to gasp.

"Should you sit, Mam?" Sarah asked sweetly. I shook my head. It was I, not her who should be composed.

Madam Sally, as she introduced herself, said Albert Todd was a customer of at least a year. The dates she gave me lined up with the "adventures" our husband took, leaving Sister Faye and I to look after business and family. She said Charles sat quietly in the lobby while his brother spent his time with prostitutes. I winced at the thought of Charles, trying to be loyal to his blood know and remembering his vows to me at the same time.

She was quite surprised to hear Albert Todd was already married. "I figured that other man must've had an allegiance." She told me with a smirk. "But not Albert. Many men fall in love with our girls. He took a special liking to Daisy Congruse. Wrote her letters when he was gone and brought special gowns when he came to visit."

Poor Faye. No wonder she was so miserable. Albert Todd had little thought of his family. Who knows if he had prior circumstances with other women?

She pulled a picture from her pocket. "These are all of my girls. I keep photos so the men can take their time choosing. No pressure," she handed me a photo of a young lass of no more than twenty. She had long, fair curls and eyes like Faye's, wide and lovely. Her leg was perched on a chair in an unseemly manner, barely concealing what should have rested under a dress. Her face looked pained; she certainly didn't want to appear in such a manner. She was holding a parasol that matched her undergarments, no doubt used as a prop in many of their photos.

I thought of my own dochter. Why would a parent allow their child to do such a thing? Madame Sally, as if reading my mind, said, "Didn't have a family, that one. Given up to an aunt and uncle as a child. When they died, she was on her own. She had to feed herself somehow. Came here as a youngster."

That's when I understood, Da. Albert Todd was trying to save her. He wanted to protect this delicate waif the way he wasn't able to protect his own Wee Hiram. The prostitutes in Aisley Lumber Township are frequently beaten and left for dead. He passed those scenes every day when he was in town. I thanked Madam Sally.

The next morning, Mr. Samuel Li had business in Astoria before we returned. Sarah and I shared apple butter sandwiches and coffee on the veranda of the hotel. While we ate, each lost in our own thoughts, a man approached us. He said he'd heard we were looking to find out about the mistress who died.

Sarah, without a hint of shame, retrieved her notebook. I nodded; a bit afraid of what might come next. He told us he owned the boat the three took out that fateful day.

"Sorry for yer loss, missus," he said, tipping his cap. "A Chinese man gave me a nice tip to come up here and tell you the story of the three who rented my boat and met an untimely end." He pulled out a chair and sat beside me, the familiar stench of dead sea life clinging to his clothes.

He said the man and woman had just married and were full of whiskey and cake. They wished to take a boat out to see the dolphins. "First, I refused. They weren't in no shape to take a boat anywhere. This ain't like no row boat on a lake. It's real sea waters. They left and came back a bit later with a tall, serious man. Pushed him in front of me and says he'll take charge of the boat. So's they can have a nice wedding-day ride. The tall man grumbled 'bout not thinking this was proper."

Sarah squeezed my hand, I'm sure happy to hear her faither disapproved. "What happened next?"

"Told 'em there was rumors of pirates and to be aware. Tall man said he always carried a pistol and patted his side. They were told, bring it back in 90 minutes. After two hours, I could see a storm on the horizon. Knew if they weren't back, they weren't comin.'"

The man paced nervously, afraid for the future of his boat and that of its occupants. When the violent storm came and passed and still no boat, he knew the fate of the three. It was the next morning when their bodies washed up.

"My best boat. Hate to complain 'bout it, what with yer deeper concerns."

I offered to pay him for the boat, but he said Mr. Samuel Li had already paid him handsomely.

As he walked away, Sarah continued scribbling furiously. "What do you think of all of this, lass?" I asked.

"My da tried to do what was right at every turn. Uncle must've been drunk and unruly so they fought. Da punched Uncle. They struggled and the gun accidentally went off. It was a horrible accident, Mam. We can put our fears to rest. We just won't tell Auntie. Her heart can't take it."

If that's what she wants to think, that's good enough for me. Twisting my thoughts into anything more won't bring them back. That's the end of things.

Your Devoted Dochter,

Fiona Flanagan Scheddy

Chapter Twenty-Three

PINEY FALLS, OREGON

I'm back at Cosmic Cakes and Antiquery. There are several people milling about, looking at antique bowls and rusty tools. Even though I've taken yearly trips to Europe to find pieces for my house, I can't get enthusiastic about domestic antiques. I am exactly the snob Dancinee said I was: more connected with dusty centerpieces than living, breathing humans.

After a few minutes, I realize there are no tantalizing smells coming from the back as is usual. There is an older lady standing at the counter, hands on hips. She is wearing her obligatory green nametag, *WELCOME TO PINEY FALLS!! I'm (this part is covered in orange tape) Ask me about hand-cut pepperoni!* In the refrigerated case is a sign that reads, "Day Old Only." Neatly stacked square muffins sit untouched.

"Where's Cosmo?" I ask.

She pushes her glasses up her nose and eyes me suspiciously. "Why do you want to know?"

"Oh, I'm a friend." I think about what Dancinee said. *He's an easy mark.* "A casual friend. I borrowed some things from him yesterday that I promised to return."

Her face softens and she smiles, revealing three gold teeth in the front. "His sister took to the road. Least that's what I'm thinking."

"Cedar is missing? Is that normal for her? To disappear?"

She shakes her head, causing the excessive skin under her chin to swing back and forth. "Not that I know of. Those two are like butter and bread. She'd tell Cos if she was gonna leave. He got up today and knocked on her door, like always, and she didn't answer. The police are there now."

I'm unsure how to proceed. "I know this is unusual, but can you tell me where she lives? I'm worried some questions I've been asking might be causing her distress."

She folds her arms across her ample chest. "Ohhh. You're the lady who's been askin' about the Flanagan sisters. Doubt that would bother her. They've been dead near a hundred years."

I'm frustrated. What does she care? "Can you please just tell me where he might be? I'm not the greatest with directions in this little town, but I can always..."

She points straight up. "Cos lives upstairs. The

door is around back. His sister lives above the building next door."

Without giving myself any more time to worry about it, I head out behind the building to the rickety stairs. In the city, no one would dare climb these without a weapon of some kind. There would be no telling what was behind the door once you reached the top.

I hesitate for a moment before knocking. No one answers. What am I doing here anyway? It's none of my business. I turn to leave and the door opens just a crack. "Who's there?" I can hear his rich voice, though weaker than it was three days ago.

"Cosmo? It's me, Lanie. I was just worried about you." I move closer and I see his eyes are rimmed red. I can smell liquor on his breath. It reminds me of the whiskey I drank before spending the night with my boss's boss. There is a knot in my stomach, but it's not Cosmo-related. It's definitely guilt. Dancinee opened a wound.

"Are you okay?" Stupid question. Of course, he isn't.

"My sister is gone. No note or anything. She's only done this once before." Tears are forming in his beautiful eyes and my heart breaks.

"Can I come in?" I ask. He opens the door wide. I don't know what I was expecting, but the apartment is clean; spotless. There are two plants with long, trailing vines covered in leaves sitting on the coffee table. The tiny kitchen is neat, no evidence a broken man is living here.

"Take your shoes off, please. It's a little quirk I have."

Obediently I remove both of my shoes and leave them on a black shag rug next to the door.

"Do you have any idea where she might be?" Now I see the bottle of whiskey sitting on his counter.

"When I was incarcerated, I didn't hear from her for almost a year. Never did find out why. She's my only family. After the cult broke up and I went to prison, my parents just took off. Never raised us in the first place. They didn't want anything to do with us, so Cedar was my only family. When you're stuck, alone like that, you really rely on whoever doesn't cut you out. Worse than being in prison, that just about broke me. After a year, she showed up one visiting day."

"Did she ever explain what was going on?" I sit down on his gray couch, pulling a red pillow onto my lap.

He takes a big swig from the bottle. "She said she was having some bad memories of our time in Fallen Branch. Zion messed with her head. Because of my trial..." he looks for my reaction. I try very hard not to have one. "She pushed all of that stuff out of the way."

"Maybe that's what she's doing now. Taking some time."

"She'll never forgive me. That's the problem."

"She could be at the falls. You told me people are drawn there in times of trouble."

"I took a hike this morning. Didn't see her."

"In this state? Was that safe?"

He stares at me. "I've got to find my sister."

"Can I make you some coffee? Things always make more sense once the alcohol has worn off. I know from experience."

He shrugs. "Okay. That's probably true. It's in the cupboard."

His coffee maker is just like the one I had in my office. I watched my assistant use it a hundred times. I wish I would have offered to help her even once. Just to make sure he is good and sober, I dump extra coffee into the filter. At least I think it's extra; I can't be sure.

I place a tall mug in front of him and take one for myself, bringing the questionable creation to my lips. It sits in my mouth for a few seconds too long before I spit it back into the cup. I watch tentatively as he takes a drink without hesitation. No reaction. I sit on the far end of the couch, suddenly conscious of any physical contact that may send him signals I shouldn't send.

"What did she say to you the last time you spoke?"

Our conversation yesterday had to have something to do with her disappearance. "What can I do?"

Cosmo abruptly begins to cry, his shoulders shaking. Without thinking, I clutch him and pull him close to me. He lays his head on my shoulder and we sit in silence.

I haven't had this kind of intimacy without expectations since my boyfriend in college. Once, I had an assistant who lost his mother and wanted a hug. I told him no and sent him home.

After several minutes, he lays down, putting his head in my lap. I picture Dancinee's look of disapproval, but I can't bring myself to push him off.

"This is the best way to think," he explains.

I start to stroke his hair and then stop myself. *This isn't one of your conquests, Lanie.*

I stare at the whiskey bottle and realize it is almost full. "You didn't drink all of this before I got here?"

"I just opened it before you came."

"Sorry, I jumped to conclusions. You shouldn't have suffered through that coffee in silence."

He clears his throat. "The prison commissary lowered my standards."

"Where do you think she might go to work things through, other than the falls?"

He lifts his head from my lap and squints. "Why didn't I figure it out sooner? He stands up abruptly, almost hitting my chin with an arm. "I know exactly where she is! I need someone to come with me, in case she is hurt and I need help."

"I'm not good with first aid or helping..." I stare into his blue eyes. The old Lanie wouldn't be so easily swayed. "Okay. I'll come."

I bend over to put my shoes on and notice something stuck to his laces. It's a green nametag. *Welcome to Piney Falls!! I'm Cosmo! Ask me about our free parking!*

"Your nametag." I point to his shoe. "I've been

wondering about those. Why does everyone have them? And some of you have them partially covered?"

"Yeah. The city council passed an ordinance a few years ago. Everyone who works in a public space has to wear these idiotic things. Supposed to help promote tourism. There are two problems with that. One, we're not that friendly. Two, there are no tourists." He smiles. "So, I wear mine here. The ordinance didn't specify exactly where we had to wear them." He grabs his jacket and we head down the stairs to the tiny, covered parking area. He walks up to a shiny, black motorcycle.

"Oh, I don't ride those." The thought of hanging on to someone else while they get to make the driving decisions without my consent is terrifying. "Don't you have a car?"

"This is my one and only mode of transportation." He looks at me pleadingly. "It's about my sister. I can't do this without you!" He doesn't wait for a response. Instead, he pulls an extra helmet from the shelf above his bike and hands it to me. It is midnight blue and covered in constellations.

I'm hesitant to put it on. I don't as a rule put anything on my hair since I spend so much to make it look the way it does. Then I realize I haven't done anything with my hair since I arrived.

Cosmo starts the engine and I try and fail to get on the back gracefully. He tips the bike slightly toward me. "Hang on to my shoulder and swing your leg over. Don't worry if it takes more than one try." He smiles.

I visualize the last conversation I had with Vem on our walk. "See what you want to be," she said to me as I was huffing and puffing my way up to Little Cone Falls. I imagine my legs to be just as long and muscular as hers. I thrust my leg in the air and miraculously it lands on the other side of the bike, after grazing Cosmo's back. "Sorry!"

As much as I don't want to, I hold on to his waist, trying to lean forward as I do.

We ride through town, turning off on a dirt road and winding around tall trees until it seems like we are hopelessly lost. I hate that I am hanging on to him so tightly. The further we go, the tighter my grip around him.

There is one more turn, this time down an even narrower road. The trees get closer together and there is nothing to see beyond them. Finally, we break out into a clearing. At the end of the road, two tall logs hold a sign over the road that announces, "Fallen Branch Community."

Chapter Twenty-Four

AISLEY LUMBER TOWNSHIP, OREGON

Dearest Da,

I decided to follow in Faye's proud steps and take the care to find a need and fill it. The school house in our community was only one room. Students took turns reading books and sitting at a desk, the other cold, wet days they sat on the floor as close to the fire as they could. Needless to say, lots of illnesses are to be had from these poor conditions. Although we teach our bairn they aren't different from others, they never had to suffer these indignities.

I commissioned employees of Mr. Stanford Aisley to construct a new building in the center of town, where one of the bars burned to the ground. I asked my workers to volunteer their time for the sake of their wee ones and they readily agreed. They chopped the trees and milled the wood, helping to erect a sturdy building.

I bought the books and hired more teachers. Each

morning before I go to the cannery, I go to the school to check on the students. Bright-eyed and eager, there are twenty-eight pupils so far. They are every color of the rainbow and all have eagerness to learn in common. I grade the school work and sometimes help prepare the noon meal. Flanagan City School is a happy place for learning. Mam would be so proud.

I've not told you about the great accomplishments of my bairn. Sarah continues to show a fascination with the hospital. She sits by the beds of patients, making them jolly and asking about their ailments. She takes notes in her notebook, able to remind the doctors of their symptoms each day.

The most exciting news for both Sarah and myself is that a woman surgeon has joined our hospital! I can barely keep Sarah away. She wants to learn everything there is to know about surgery, and the privilege to achieve this from a woman is a great honor. Sarah came home one day and excitedly told the story of watching Dr. Julebon at work. She performed surgery on a poor lass thought to be the longest case of gestation in the country. Her belly was swollen for almost two years. The surgeon found a large tumor and with her nimble, skilled fingers, removed it. When placed on the scale, it weighed an impressive eighteen pounds!

At age fifteen, most young ladies have their coming out receptions in a large city. Mrs. Aisley took her daughter to San Francisco for the grand event. Though Charles and I never discussed it specifically, we both felt Sarah should live a humble life. Sarah seems indifferent about the prospects of marriage. She wants instead to continue her education.

Walter at age ten is the tallest and smartest in his class. He is eager to learn more of the cannery and of life beyond our little town. I fear he will be the first to leave us to explore, just like his faither. His hair is the color of sunset, just like yours Da.

Walter and Shaw both attend Flanagan City School. They are precocious boys, always finding a way to help when they can and get in trouble when they can't. One day when I came to walk home with them, Miss Treadwith asked if we had stained glass windows at home.

As a belated wedding gift, Charles commissioned a fine stained-glass window to be made, overlooking the second-floor landing. It contains pink glass in the shape of a Thistle flower. As the children grew older, I would tell them stories of my homeland and the victory against England at the Battle of Bannockburn in 1314, led by Robert the Bruce. They came to know and love Scotland through the beautiful symbol left us by their dear faither.

The boys were telling the familiar story to classmates one day and the other students thought them to be lying. "Well," Shaw says, "we shall make a stained-glass window here, just for you all to enjoy." The boys found my paints and brought them to school without my knowledge. I sent them early to school many days to work on their math and stoke the furnace before the teacher arrived.

They took it upon themselves to paint a fine likeness of the ocean and a fishing boat. When the other students arrived, Samuel proudly stood and asked other students to tell their stories of origin as they looked at the window.

I didn't know whether to punish them or hug them. Boys with a big heart they are. I told the teacher I would talk to Faye about getting their own stained-glass window. She readily agreed and we ordered a fine window from a business in Seattle, a German glass maker who fashioned a window with a fishing boat design. Even on the rainiest days, there is light coming into the classroom thanks to my boys.

Lachlan Douglas has become intolerable. Just last week he fired Mr. Jonah Li, brother of Samuel, and new employee, for laughing at a joke told by another man while on break. Lachlan Douglas says there is to be no merriment in the workplace and had the poor man taken from the cannery and only given a half-day's pay.

He, just as Samuel before him, is trying to make enough to bring more family members to our country. When Mr. Samuel Li came to tell me of his misfortune, I hired Mr. Jonah Li immediately to clean floors at the hospital.

Lachlan Douglas also ended our monthly employee dinners, insisting the space be used as paid storage for another cannery. It does make us more money, I'll admit. I can't help but think it is helpful, especially to the men without families, to have time of enjoyment when they aren't drowning in bloody fish.

Anything he demands, Sister Faye readily supports. She was never so agreeable with her husband. They argued over the color of the sky and the names of their bairn when neither could remember.

This can't go on, and I'm secretly looking for another man to take over his position. Well, not the position he THINKS he has, but the one we hired him for. I don't want my own boys to be subject to his environment when it comes time for them to take over the running of the family business.

Mr. Samuel Li reminds me that we take advantage of the situation we have, not the one we want. Soon, he says, things will change.

Enough of my unpleasant thoughts.
Your Devoted Dochter,
Fiona Flanagan Scheddy

Chapter Twenty-Five

PINEY FALLS, OREGON

We pull into the campground, over a very bumpy road that has almost been reclaimed by nature. There are four long buildings that have fallen into disrepair. Many years ago, it looks like they were painted yellow. The structures form a square and in the middle is a large pit. I can see a woman sitting on the far edge of the pit. Cedar.

We stop and I'm hesitant to get off. My legs have settled into this awkward position and aren't likely to change easily. Cosmo notices me struggling. "Step on the peg and swing your leg high again. Do it in one motion so you don't have to think about it!" He yells over the sound of his obnoxiously loud motor. Like Vem's high-kicks in the forest when she's doing...I don't know what she's doing. I lean on his shoulder and awkwardly fight my way to the ground, feeling an embarrassed sense of accomplishment. He turns off the motor and gets off with ease.

I can tell he is anxious to see his sister. "Go! I'll catch up." I try to hold my thighs in place with my arms.

He runs to Cedar and sits beside her, holding her tightly. It looks strange to me, but I've avoided relationships of any kind my entire life. Maybe this is normal? I hesitate, both for the sake of my legs and the fact that I'm unsure of whether I should be observing. They are still in this pose when I walk up gingerly behind them.

"My sweet Cedar," Cosmo releases his sister and cups her chin tenderly. "Why didn't you tell me where you were? You know I don't breathe out unless you're nearby to catch it. "

"I had some bad memories come back yesterday. Things that hadn't been on my mind for years. Cos, I tried to keep this inside forever, but I don't think I should. I came out here to figure out how to tell you."

I inch slightly closer.

"Why would you keep things from me, sis? I thought we didn't have secrets?"

"It didn't seem worth hurting you. You've been through enough all of these years." She points over her head, towards me. "She came in yesterday. Made me uncomfortable, trying to get me to talk about some things. She's nosey and kind of pushy."

Cosmo turns sharply. "Didn't you say you were

here to learn about the Flanagan sisters? Why would you bother Cedar about personal stuff?"

My cheeks turn bright red. "I...uh... I didn't mean to pry." *Yes, I did.* "I figured there was some relation between Fallen Branch and the reason Flanagan changed to Piney Falls."

Cosmo stands up and walks toward me in a menacing manner. He's acting as though he might strike me. I've never been afraid of a man before and I'm not going to start today. I push my chest out and stare him down.

"This isn't about her, Cos. She said something that really made me think. Do I want to continue to be a follower after all of these years, or do I want to lead? That's what this is about. Me taking charge. Come sit."

He turns reluctantly and rejoins her on the ground.

"Zion shared lots of things with me. I was the only other person to hold a key to his Box of Intellect; all of the secrets of the world, he said, somehow contained within a wooden box. It's hard to imagine the story of the universe is in a box with a smiley face carved on top." She rolls her eyes.

"All the financial information too," Cedar continues. So many wealthy people came to join our group from all over the world. He charged them hundreds of thousands of dollars for the privilege of experiencing his way of life. That's how we functioned. It wasn't because we were self-supporting by making all of those stupid little crafts and selling vegetables in town."

"I figured that one out before my tenth birthday." Cosmo wraps his arms around one knee. "Is that it?"

"Like I said, he told me lots of things. He drank at night and that's when he'd really get loose-lipped. One night he started talking about all the kids in the group. How some of them were just imbeciles who wouldn't grow up to do anything important? But he knew I would be someone special."

"You were his favorite, so he wanted to make sure you were happy enough to stay with him," I interject. They both turn and frown at me.

Cedar takes Cosmo's hand in hers. "Brother, one night as he was blathering on about someone's clumsiness, he blurted out, 'My children will never be caught stumbling down the road.' I thought because he was drunk, he just babbled. By then, it was three in the morning and I just wanted to go to bed because I knew he'd make me get up at seven and start my chores."

I have taken a seat behind them, my inner thighs now screaming in discomfort from the long ride. It may be awhile before I can stand properly again.

"I was irritated," Cedar continues, "so I said, 'You don't have any kids, Zion. You've never even been with a woman.'" Cedar looks off in the distance. "I could say things like that to him. He never punished me the way he did others when they were insolent. That's when he told me the truth." She pauses for a moment. "That he did have a child. Me."

Cosmo leans back. "You're my twin. How could that be? Our mother wasn't with Zion. Or maybe she was?"

"Oh, Cos. This is so hard." Cedar takes in a few shallow breaths and lets them out slowly. "We don't share a mother but we do share a father. That's what he told me that night. You and I were both the result of his relationships, but we had different mothers."

"No. That's not right." Cosmo shakes his head.

"Two babies were born to two different women he slept with, both born on the same day. He was controlling every story in the camp–he made the decision we would be raised as twins. The woman, your mother, left the group shortly after you were born. Never seen again."

Cosmo pushes her hand away. "What? You can't be serious. Why would you be telling me this now?" He stands up and rubs his chin. "He can't be my... our... father. Why would you wait until now to admit this?"

He stands up and rubs the back of his neck. "No, sis, you're wrong on this one. We've shared everything our whole lives. Like two peas. Sometimes we didn't even have to talk. We just sensed each other."

She stands as well, trying to put her arms around his waist but he moves away. "We're brother and sister. And we went through something awful together. None of that has changed. I found out the night before the city council meeting. I decided I'd tell you the next day, but...everything happened so quickly.

After you were sent to prison, I vowed I'd keep this secret forever. You'd been through enough."

"Then SHE came in." She looks at me warily. "The way she went about things was wrong, but her message was right. I needed to get this out in the open. It's been my master for too long."

"I talked to our father - well, the man I thought was our father - six times. I remember each of them." Cosmo's voice is shaky. "One time after he came out of Zion's quarters. I was on my way to weed the corn. Do you remember how much I hated that?"

Cedar nods.

"That day was so hot," Cosmo continues, "I would have done anything to avoid that humid, smothering space. When he called me over, I was more excited about avoiding the sun than having a conversation with my own dad." Cosmo sighs. "The man we assumed was our father."

"I remember your telling me about that, Cos. I talked to Dad that day, too." Cedar stares as if she's in another time. "He asked me to meet him behind that building over there," She is pointing to a long, narrow windowless building, evidently for my benefit. It looks like a prison. "That's where we used to do laundry. He told me that he cared very much for me, and couldn't believe how I had grown. Then, he pulled up his sleeve to show me his scar. It was recent, still angry and red. It was in the shape of a 'Z'. He was proud of it.

"Zion branded him? Did he do that to everyone?" I interrupt.

"No," Cedar continues. "Just people who he thought needed extra help staying in line. Dad said he went to Zion a few times asking to see us. That was Zion's response. He told him if there was more insubordination, he would just remove that limb altogether."

She moves to Cosmo's side once more, resting her head on his shoulder.

"Do you think he knew that you weren't his? As crazy as this place was, maybe they just told him his wife gave birth to twins and he accepted it." He begins to cry.

"I don't know for sure, Cos. At least he tried that one time to be with us."

"I'm going to go stand by the motorcycle," I announce. As I walk back, I can hear them whispering.

I look around at the dilapidated buildings. I can see one of them says "Gathering Hall" above it. I wonder how many hours Cosmo and Cedar spent listening to Zion, their father, making up some ridiculous story. Watching in the same building but across the room from the people they knew as their parents. How painful that must have been for them both. Directly across from me is a sign that says, "Nutrition and Educa." The rest of the sign has been burned off. Cosmo? Or some other angry former member? There is an eeriness to this whole place. It feels like an abrupt ending where souls still wander, looking for something never to be found.

It's possible that's the real story. The cult. I could

just give up on the story of Flanagan's ending. I still haven't come up with any of the information I came here to get. Now that I think about it, it was ridiculous to drive halfway across the country to search for answers to a story that nobody but me cares about.

This town is blanketed in mystery; so what? I don't see people tripping over themselves to figure out why. It's time to go back to reality. Find a new job. This time I'll do something more meaningful. Hire employees and treat them as humans. It's time I change for the better.

I breathe in deeply, inhaling the smell of evergreen trees and the salt of the ocean air. I open my arms like Vem taught me and close my eyes while I breathe in deeply. My mind calms and clears.

"Lanie?" Cosmo and Cedar are holding hands standing right behind me. I didn't even hear them. This meditation business really works.

"Didn't you learn not to sneak up on people in all of your years in this creepy place?"

They look at each other and Cedar nods. "We've made a decision about something. You came here for information. It's unfair of us to keep it from you. Tomorrow we'll meet in Cosmo's Bakery and tell you everything we know."

Chapter Twenty-Six

AISLEY LUMBER TOWNSHIP, OREGON

Dearest Da,

You have been my safe place to confess all of my life. Do you remember when I dug in your dresser drawer and found the sgian-dubh passed from father tae son? I wanted to hold it so badly. To understand what it felt like to have that connection to our long past relatives. I dropped it promptly on the hardwood floor. Even though I knew it would mean a beating, I showed you the knife with its chipped handle.

Instead of lecturing, you took me in your arms and promised you'd always love your girls just as much as their brothers. You hugged me and promised it'd be our secret. I don't know if Mam ever figured it out. Wasn't but a year before she passed.

I've always held guilt over that. It was the one thing you were proudest to own. I couldn't hardly believe when you gave it to us as a wedding gift, instead of saving it for our male know. Now as then, I've done something awful and you're the only one I care to share this burden with.

Lachlan Douglas has gone about his new life as though he is the third Scheddy brother. He makes decisions about the cannery as if he's in soul ownership. After all the canning is done for the season, we do a thorough cleaning of the premises. One night I struggled to sleep and noticed lights on in the cannery building. Since we were almost done with our cleaning, I knew there wasn't anyone who should be there.

Walter accompanied me with his very own shotgun, purchased for hunting season. We were surprised to see Lachlan Douglas and several new employees, sitting 'round a table with cards. Walter bravely pointed his gun ahead of me as I marched into the room. I demanded to know what was happening in MY establishment. There are, after all, many places men can go to gamble and commit all sorts of transgressions. There is no need to use our honest place of business for such disgusting habits.

Lachlan Douglas smiled his devilish smile and told me to go home, he was conducting business. I refused to leave and the longer I stood there, the more I realized these men were not in their right minds. Four men - three Chinese and one Finnish - swayed in their seats, looking as though they hadn't had a good night's sleep in weeks.

As Lachlan Douglas was insisting we leave, ignoring Walter's demands that he do the same, two other men entered. With them they carried large sacks. They didn't seem to mind the presence of a woman as they pulled the sacks over the swaying men and began removing them from the premises.

The story finally came out. Lachlan Douglas had contracted with these criminals to entice our former employees in for a night of gambling and liquor. Upon their extreme intoxication, the men would be removed and taken aboard large ships to be used as labor for the period of a year.

"To pay off their gambling debt," Lachlan Douglas insisted.

"How long have you been doing this?"

"Near six months. Faye is aware."

I couldn't believe my ears. Walter's eyes widened. Happening under my nose and I had no idea. I did the payroll for employees. There was a turnover of men each year, but it's hard work. One must be deft with a large knife and unafraid of the strang smells of fish and death. To think the place we worked so hard to build with our own hands had become a harbor for a kidnapper was too much.

I threatened first to inform the authorities. Lachlan Douglas laughed, reminding me I was also in the wrong, making a contract with him to act as a facade for the true owners. He also mentioned he spent many nights in the saloon with the chief constable, they were good friends.

"We'll end the contract. I'll pay for your early

release." I had enough money to pay him off. More than I could ever spend.

"I'm not going anywhere. I'm going to marry Faye. She'll sign her portion of the business over to me just as soon as we've sealed our marriage. Face it, Fiona, I've outplayed you."

Walter pointed his weapon dead center on Lachlan Douglas's brow. "There'll be no bloodshed on my account." I pushed the gun to his side.

Walter and I slunk back to our home, feeling defeated. This wasn't the life Charles and I planned. I couldn't leave the cannery, or whatever it was now, to the boys as I'd always dreamed. My sons are good farmers, hard workers. They don't mind milking the cows in the morning or planting and harvesting vegetables at the end of the summer. I could sell my share of the cannery to someone else.

I didn't want to talk to Faye about it. What would she say? She was blinded by love, maybe the first real love she felt in her life. I would have to handle this myself. I thought long and hard as I painted what I remembered of Charles' lovely face: Walter's stubborn chin, Simon's deep-set eyes, and Sarah's big ears. Out of one man came three strang, merry children. I had to do something.

The next day, Mrs. Aisley was surprised to see me. Of late, we haven't socialized much. She gave up on trying to make me a San Francisco socialite. She feels Sarah won't be accepted as a proper woman in society, won't be able to find a husband of means, unless she is presented. Sarah has been adamant she is not going to be a society woman and will find a suitable husband when and if she deems it necessary for her survival.

We drank our Earl Gray tea in silence as I worked up the nerve to tell her of the shady goings on at the cannery. I remembered the first day in town, looking at her as if she were royalty sitting in her very own American castle. Now all these years later, I live in a bigger home than she does and can easily see through the cracks in her purely social soul. She excels beyond me in one important area: hiding her true feelings.

It made me need to confess my sins all the more. She and I were alike now - each accomplishing what was needed, no matter what the cost. Neither came through our years in Aisley Lumber Township unscathed, and she seemed to enjoy when I made mistakes so she didn't feel so alone. She encouraged and goaded me until I broke down and began this sordid tale. Once it began, I couldn't stop the words from pouring out, all over her rose-covered china. It mattered little that in a mere few hours, all of her local friends would know my business. There is a power in the ability to keep one's emotions as hidden as our womanly form. A power I don't possess.

It wasn't just the story of Lachlan Douglas that ran out of my mouth like a river, but also the worries of the past two years without my husband. How I questioned every decision I made, worried that it wouldn't honor my husband in some way. I tried to be a good wife, even when I was doing bad things. I reasoned Charles would have understood.

"I just need him removed. Our lives will return to normal if he is elsewhere." I pictured him working unhappily in Mr. Stanford Aisley's Seattle lumber mill. There was no room for guilt.

I let my emotions take hold and soon Mrs. Aisley pressed her fine linen to my cheek and patted my hand. She couldn't contain her glee. "I'll take care of everything, dear," she assured me. "We women feel trapped, don't we? The only way to better ourselves is by helping each other."

Do you remember the farm hand you hired the summer of Faye's thirteenth year, Da? You caught him stabbing at the legs of the sheep and we knew him to be a bad bodie. The boys weren't strang enough to lift the bales, so we had to keep him. Then you caught him in the barn, pressed up against Wee Faye, pushing the scythe against her tiny neck.

When I asked what happened to our farm hand, you explained to me that, 'Things 'at must be dain whether we want tae or nae.' I understood, Da. Things have to be taken care of. I've set in motion something that can't be undone. It main be dain.

Your Devoted Dochter,

Fiona Flanagan Scheddy

Chapter Twenty-Seven

PINEY FALLS, OREGON

"I can't, Vem. I've got to meet Cosmo and Cedar. They're going to give me what I need to write this damned story." I transfer my weight to the other slippered foot. "My time here is almost up and I haven't written one word. That was my goal, after all. These weeks have to mean something." They mean something. A new Lanie.

November Bean is standing in my doorway, hands on hips. The color of the day is rust. From scrunchy to shoes. "You have to center yourself first, Lanie. Haven't you learned anything from me in our time together?"

She is like steel: impenetrable. I doubt my ability to move her even if I had the physical strength. "You would be a powerhouse in the business world. You could make millions doing seminars on the power of standing in the way." I chuckle, hoping to break her serious gaze, but she continues boring a hole through me, not even breathing. "Okay, you win." I find my coat and put on my shoes, the sneakers I found in the back of a closet. "But we have to be quick."

We head up the usual pathway, and then she stops, thunking me on the shoulder. "You wanted to see the old Flanagan place, right? It's up this way." She points to a piece of ground that doesn't have an obvious path.

"Where?"

"There!" She takes my head in her hands and points to the same area again. Outside of this town, no one would get away with that.

"Opportunities are always there, if you are quiet enough to witness them."

I've grown used to her nonsensical thoughts. Sometimes they actually make sense. I stand, motionless. The more I stare, the more I can see places the tree branches are broken, a forgotten path that still bears small signs of use.

"Is this something I can actually do? You know I'm not—"

"Sometimes you can just let things happen without controlling them."

Has she been talking to Dancinee?

"I'll give it a try. That's all I can promise." I let Vem go first, trying to push away my fear of wild animals popping out from behind these untamed branches.

"The more I discover about this place, the more I want to know," I say nervously, more for my distraction than conversation. Keep talking, I think, so I can remain calm in case a wild hairy beast bursts from the weeds and gnaws off my leg. "What we might learn from the Flanagan sisters today."

Vem is uncharacteristically quiet. It is steep and I'm ready to turn around.

"Do you want to see where they're buried? It's not far."

"The Scheddys?" I'm trying to catch my breath. "I would love to."

"Almost there," Vem calls back. "It's up on top of this hill." She bursts through a set of weeds to a space where only the foundation of a house stands. "This is where Faye and Fiona lived the last years of their lives. The place burned to the ground shortly after the demise of Fallen Branch. Some say it was the spirits of the two women, tired of the gawkers coming to stare at their tragedy."

I look at the foundation and feel ill. A house that was most likely a showpiece, reduced to a few cement blocks in the ground. I walk around the perimeter, trying to gauge the size.

"It's just about the size of mine. Was. The size mine was."

"You haven't released that yet, have you?"

I don't have to turn around and look at her. I know she's standing with her arms crossed, expecting I'll tell her my deepest, darkest fears. How the house was my entire identity. "It's released, Vem. The house is gone. My life is starting over."

"Starting over takes more than a new house," she begins. "It's finding your new purpose, whatever that may be. And figuring out who you are, underneath all of your expensive subterfuge."

"That's all I am, unfortunately." I didn't mean to let that slip.

"No, Lanie. I can see you. I mean really see you. The reason you're drawn to Cosmo. You're both so afraid to let people in and be a little vulnerable."

Even though we're outside, the air seems to have disappeared. "You don't know who I am," I whisper, tucking my hands underneath my arms.

"You were drawn here for a purpose. I know it. We'll do a chant—"

"What do you think?" I interrupt. "About the Flanagan fire?"

She shrugs. "It was probably some kids messing around." She pulls at the corners of her mouth. "More likely it was former Fallen Branch members, escaped from the hell of that commune and trying to take their anger out on something."

I nod, relieved she was distracted so easily. I notice there are ornaments of some type left in each blackened corner.

"See? I told you. Fallen Branch. Those are the identification medallions."

I walk gingerly to a corner and pick one up. It is a large tree with many tendrils snaking out from the bottom. Roots gone wild. "Whose was this?" I ask, holding it out to Vem.

She takes it from my hand and studies it for a

minute. "It's some joker. Not a real Fallen Branch member."

"How do you know?"

"Because that's Zion's symbol. Remember the medallion you found the other day? Similar, but a cheap imitation. All of our medallions were made from Hemlock and covered in some kind of epoxy. This is a bored kid who carved a basic picture without putting on any kind of sealant. Amateur." She sniffs and tosses it back on the ground.

I look around, trying to picture the kids from the photographs playing hide-and-seek between the giant trees.

"Why are these trees shorter?"

"That's where they grew vegetables for the hospital. At one point, there were no trees here at all. The land tends to reclaim itself when the humans are gone. Plants know how to start over better than humans."

We take a sharp turn to the left, where a formidable home still stands. Red paint flecks dot the gray wood, bare and exposed. It looks like something out of a horror film, with a shaky porch surrounding the front of the building. There are broken windows two stories up. Three black shutters hang by one nail.

There is a gold plaque, covered in fluorescent orange spray paint. *Former Home of Flanagan Lane Hospital. 1921-1950.*

More than 1,000 patients passed through these doors

I'm horrified. "Why is this in such disrepair?"

"I dunno. Maybe because this town likes to pretend like the Flanagan sisters never existed."

"Why?"

"Isn't that what you came to figure out? I don't have all the answers, Lanie."

We climb just a little higher, to another flat spot. There are two giant trees shading five, large, flat stones standing tall in the sea of trees. I read each of them: *Charles Scheddy, Beloved Brother, Faither, Husband and Businessman.* There is one for his brother, Albert Todd, simply stating his name and date of death. Beside him is Faye and beside her, Fiona. There is a small tombstone that reads *Wee Hiram Scheddy, beloved son of Fay and Albert Todd.*

I bend down and touch each one.

"Trying to sense their spirit?" Vem asks.

"Something like that."

"Close your eyes and just listen."

I do as she asks and I feel a sadness. I pull my hand away.

Chapter Twenty-Eight

AISLEY LUMBER TOWNSHIP, OREGON

Dearest Da,

One night, Faye banged on my door at half past twelve. "He's gone," she cried, hair covering her bonnie blue eyes. I put my arm around her and settled her in for a cup of tea, while she prattled on about Lachlan Douglas going out for his evening constitution as he always did. I stared hard at my sister. How could she think I was so daft as to not realize what he was really doing? I didn't say a word about it though. This wasn't the time for arguments about something that was now in the past.

"He's always home by now. We have a ritual," she said shyly.

I put my hand up. "No, Sister. I don't want to hear about your bedroom ways. It isn't proper and—"

"It's not that. Every night before bed, he bends a knee to the floor and kisses my hand. He tells me I'm the bonniest hen in the world. I can't go to sleep until he does."

For a moment I felt terrible about what I'd done. Sent him off to God knows where, to find himself another poor widow to take liberties with. But it wasn't my dear Sister Faye he would be kissing. And now she was distraught and alone once more. How much could her poor soul take? Was it the right choice?

For her bairn, for my bairn, I think it was. I pulled my nightgown up and put my knee on the cold floor. "Faye, you are the most beautiful woman in the world. I've always been jealous of your beauty." I kissed her hand.

She touched my hair and sobbed. "Oh Sister, thank you." We held in embrace for some time until she had calmed. I sent her off to bed, promising Lachlan Douglas would return before she opened her eyes in the morning.

Oh Da. I'm an awful sister. The truth of the matter is that once I sat down and thought about things for a while, I was quite relieved. To have this stranger gone from our home, from our dinner table where he kicked the children if they spoke out of turn or when he was talking about himself, as he always did, was a relief. Thinking about running things our way without his interference brought pure joy to my heart.

The next morning Faye didn't come down to breakfast. I sent Padrug up to check on her and he said his mother wouldn't be getting out of bed.

Though my touch and words of support would have done much to bring her out of her darkness, I was feeling too much guilt to let her see my face. I had work to be done, book work to finish for the cannery and without Lachlan Douglas's reproachful gaze, it would be done in a jovial mood.

After the bairn were off to their school, I walked happily to the cannery. It didn't matter that the cold rain was soaking through my coat, or that my boots were filling with the liquid and my three layers of socks would need to dry by the stove when I arrived.

I removed my dress, stockings and coat, feeling a little naughty. I could spend the day blissfully silent, without my clothing if I wished. After making a cup of tea, I sat down at the desk, my desk, and removed every notion that Lachlan Douglas ever existed in our lives. I threw out all of his things: a fine fountain pen and ink that would have been most agreeable to my daily writing but had the touch of a monstrous man, a pair of glasses, and several cigars confiscated from the Irish men for Lachlan Douglas's own pleasure.

When I returned to my office, a stranger was standing in front of the fire. His dark hair stunk like Albert Todd's Brilliantine hair oil and his beady eyes pierced through my bare skin. I reached for my knife on the desk, but he picked it up and held it at arm's length. "What kind of establishment do you think we're running?" He seized my dress from its place in front of the stove and put it to his nose. He smelled it slowly, deeply. A chill ran from my head down to my toes.

I demanded that he leave, but he announced he was the man hired by Mr. Stanford Aisley to run our cannery now that Lachlan Douglas had been "disposed of."

"What does that mean?" I snickered. "He's only moved down the road some."

The man clasped his hands together in front of him. I could see long fingernails that hadn't been cleaned. "Mr. Douglas doesn't walk this earth anymore. I saw to that. Mr. Aisley offered me the use of this building to can and ship his product."

This didn't make any sense to me. "He cuts lumber. What could he can?"

"Mushrooms. Psydrofin, to be exact. This miracle product soothes human and beast alike. They will be canned, using your label and sent to China. On the ship's return we'll be receiving opium."

My head was swirling. "How can this be done? It's illegal. Someone will discover it, surely."

He chuckled with such force it made my skin crawl. "Things are only illegal when there's someone to declare it so. We've paid off everyone we need. And you, Mrs. Scheddy, will have a fine profit from the use of your building. You can go about your social activities and we'll work in the evenings."

"What if I say no?" I asked boldly. "It is my property. Mine and my sister Faye's."

He removed a folded paper from his waste pocket.

"You've signed a document leasing the space to us. You and your sister. Lovely handwriting, both of you."

I picked up my dress off the floor and stormed out, unable to think of the words I needed. One more indignity suffered at the hands of an evil man. There is a bottomless well of them in this town, Da.

When I was composed, I went to the Aisley mansion and banged on the door. Fortunately, Mrs. Aisley answered. Though her trunks were packed she had not left for the winter yet. Flushed-cheeked I told her about what had transpired.

I was hoping for words of comfort, even if they would be reused in her society circles as a means to gossip about our small town. Instead, she sat perfectly still. "What did you expect? You asked for my husband's help and you got it. No more Mr. Douglas to give your sister a reputation. You'll make more money than your husband ever could. I don't see that you've got a problem, dearie."

It was too much. She was too much. I ran from their home to ours. Faye having just rousted herself from bed, was drinking tea in the kitchen, still wearing her night clothes. She seemed shocked by my rumpled clothing and wild-eyed demeanor, as I am always in control of my emotions.

There was no time to be polite or concern myself with her feelings. I told her what I could, taking care to re-word the deal I made to rid us of Lachlan Douglas. Instead, I confessed to her that I asked for his temporary transfer, to a lumber mill Mr. Stanford Aisley owned in Astoria. "To give us time to compose ourselves is all," I added. She was emotionless, much like Mrs. Aisley.

"Sister, you've been so busy," she finally commented, sipping her tea. "You'll have plenty of time tae rest yer body an' soul. Maybe you can work on your art."

She got up and left the room and I've not spoken to her since. We're going on ten days now. I'm not sure what to do about the mess I've created. I get up at night and see the lights on in the cannery and my stomach rolls like the grand storm at sea that claimed my dear Charles.

I'll have to try and speak to Mr. Stanford Aisley, though it seems rather pointless. He is in control now, of everything. I thought we could make our business something generations of Scheddys would be proud of. It turns out we are just women. Women without power.

Maybe you can think of something, Da. You've always been so good at coming up with a rational thought. Remember the time Brother Himey got caught in the fence? Twist one way and he'd cut his head clean off, twist the other and he'd be stuck further? You had to go in the house and think on that one, have your cup of tea and smoke.

You came back out and stood on the fence. We thought you were crazy. You pushed one way with your feet and the other with your hands. Brother Shane and I pulled him out and he was none the worse for wear. The neighbors who gathered clapped their hands at your genius.

Mr. Samuel Li came to see us, asking to use whatever potatoes are left from the harvest. He has stomach pains that will be eased by a Chinese remedy he will create. Normally, I don't burden him with our troubles. Though he has surely seen the lights burning in the cannery into the night, he hasn't said a word.

With his bounty in a sack over his shoulder, he knocked on our door. "Shi shi, Mrs. Scheddy," he said. He taught the bairn that meant "thank you" in his native language long ago. He continued to stand in the doorway and I asked if he wanted to stay for supper. He shook his head. "Long ago, I told you I would carry your burdens until it was time for you to take over. Now is the time, Fiona. Take your pack and carry it the rest of the way."

"Whatever do you mean?" I asked, not so innocently.

He shrugged and turned to leave.

I need a fence pusher now, Da.

Your Devoted Dochter,

Fiona Flanagan Scheddy

"During his endless sermons," Cedar begins, "we learned everything about his life."

"Not sermons, mind-awakening sessions," Cosmo corrects. The jingling bell over the door of Cosmic Cakes and Antiquery is constantly ringing with customers coming in and out. Cosmo walks over and pulls it down. "Never liked that sound," he remarks.

Cedar nods. "During his endless mind-awakening sessions, Zion always began at his beginning. Even though we weren't allowed to have any family connections, he made sure we learned of his." Cedar leans back in her chair and puts her arm behind it. "It's just nauseating that I remember every word."

"You had no way of blocking it out, sis," Cosmo insists. "He made sure we absorbed it all just like a poison bath."

"What did he tell you, then?" I take a bite of the

Apple Aquilla Pear Muffin in front of me. My frothy coffee arrives soon after.

"Oh, let's see... he was born in his mother's home with his grandmother assisting. His father was mentally ill and was committed to an insane asylum before he was born. I don't know if they were married."

"They weren't married," Cosmo chimes in. "That's why he didn't believe in marriage. He encouraged married couples to split up."

"No one wanted him around as a kid. His mother eventually married a man who hated him for being the son of someone who was mentally ill. Zion was a social embarrassment to his stepfather. His mother had four more children with this man. She decided Zion WAS a liability, so shortly after his fourteenth birthday, she kicked him out." Cedar stares at me, as if waiting for a reaction.

"How did he end up in Piney Falls?"

"He had relatives here. A great-uncle. Zion got a job at one of the canneries. Could debone a salmon in two minutes, he used to say." She rolls her eyes.

I take a sip of my coffee. I wonder if I lived here if I would get tired of this foamy delight. Doubtful. "How did he start the commune?"

"I don't believe any of this," Cosmo begins. "He said he went to the top of Piney Falls and confessed his desire to kill his mother for kicking him out. He says he received a sign that he should create a society where all were welcome, no one turned away. You-Top-EE-AAH.”

I open my mouth.

“That's utopia,” Cedar blessedly corrects him before I speak.

“That's why Fallen Branch members went up to the top of Piney Falls? That makes sense.”

“Yes, he wanted to make sure he was there with them, in case they had some kind of epiphany. He didn't want to miss any sign that things could be different,” Cosmo sits back and puts his hands around one knee.

“Or that someone might get a sign that Zion was absolutely crazy,” Cedar adds.

“Just former Fallen Branch members,” Cosmo adds.

“Well that would certainly make more sense than everyone just deciding they don't like the color of the sky and becoming floaters.” I regret saying that immediately. “Sorry, that is insensitive.”

“No, you're right.” Cedar concedes. “It really hurts tourism when we have so many people dying.”

I want to add that there are so many things wrong with their idea of a tourism campaign. Instead I take another sip of my coffee.

“There's one more thing. I have these other photos of the cannery workers with Faye and Fiona. It was taken some time after the deaths of their husbands.” She hands me two photos. The women are smiling.

Each have an arm locked with a male employee, so brazen.

"What caused their husband's deaths?"

"They were out in a boat for the afternoon and it capsized during a storm. Very common then. Bodies used to wash up on the beach so often they didn't think twice about it."

One of the bakers appears from the back of the store. "Cosmo, phone call. You wanna take it, or should I tell them to call back?"

"No, I'll get it. We've gone through the important stuff."

When he is gone, Cedar leans in close. "I know Cos has feelings for you," she whispers.

I want to giggle. This feels like grade school when I specifically told certain people not to tell Allen Gripper I had a crush on him, because I knew they would tell him.

"You don't have to worry. I won't..."

"You need to know: he's never dated." She sits back upright.

"Ever?" I thought those people were more like unicorns than real beings.

"Dating was forbidden in Fallen Branch. He went away to prison and then worked to get his business going when he was released. He never trusted anyone around here. Townies made fun of us; former Fallen Branch were just as messed up as he was. No one piqued his interest. Until you."

Dancinee was wrong. I won't take advantage of

Cosmo. Especially knowing he's never loved before. I'm not capable of what he deserves.

"Thanks for telling me, Cedar. You don't have to worry; I won't hurt him. He's a lovely person who has experienced enough hurt already." I don't meet her gaze. Instead, something catches my eye on the wall of the antique side of Cosmic Cakes and Antiquery.

Chapter Thirty

AISLEY LUMBER TOWNSHIP, OREGON

Dearest Da,

Maybe I was wrong about Lachlan Douglas. He did make Sister Faye very happy. I could have tolerated him, and the bairn did need a faither, no matter how stern. The grass is always greener on the other side of the fence. *Nach gorm na cnuic a tha fada bhuainn.*

These are the things I think about while I'm painting. I've all but locked myself away in my bedroom. Sarah tends to the boys since the nanny we hired thought them too disobedient. I only come out when I hear quiet, lest I encounter Sister Faye.

We rarely speak to each other, more than pleasantries meant to fool the bairn. They aren't stupid. Sarah asked me when we shall be moving away from Auntie, as she feels the chill. I dare not tell her what's really happening.

I don't believe Sister Faye to be in her right mind.

Last week I saw her clothes-pinning money to the laundry line. The week before, near midnight she stood in the yard without a stitch of clothing, *singing Hush Ye, My Bairnie. Hush ye, my bairnie, bonny wee laddie, when you're a man, you shall follow your daddie.* You remember, don't you Da? You sang it to us when we couldn't sleep.

I was afraid those unable to sleep at the hospital might catch an eyeful of her, so I sent Sarah to cover her auntie with a blanket and bring her in. Faye frequently calls her children by names of workers we once had. She even dared to call Padrug by the name of Lachlan for a week. Poor boy cried from confusion and the Mam who doesn't seem to exist.

There is a deadness in her eyes. I don't believe that this time the light will return. She has suffered too much. Some of it is at my hand and for that, I am truly sorry. It's not that I miss Lachlan Douglas around the house. We all breathe easier without his authority.

The bairn, especially, don't have to worry about tiptoeing around to avoid one of his fiery moods or lengthy lectures on whatever he deemed important that day. He would yell for hours as Faye sat by the fire, staring at something that wasn't there and the children cowered in their rooms. Maybe she started this journey into madness long ago and I wasn't willing to pay attention. Faye doesn't speak much, other than to tell anyone close by that she wishes to die. "Don't say that 'round your bairns," I admonish. It does no good, because she's not speaking to anyone in particular.

On one issue, we have full agreement. I've been using the name Flanagan, just like Faye. With the unsavory happenings at the cannery, I want my name to remain above reproach. While Faye insists Padrug and Percival use the name Flanagan as if they're Da never existed, I tell mine they can continue to be proud Scheddys. Let them keep that piece of their faither for now.

Mr. Stanford Aisley insisted that Sister Faye and I help with labels during the day, as the women who have worked for us for nearly nine years now aren't trusted to keep the true nature of the canning operations quiet. I agreed to go, separate from Sister Faye.

I hadn't labeled cans since our first days. I used to enjoy the work, prattling on with Faye about something silly one of the bairn had done, or about a tall tale we heard one of the salty Norwegian fishermen telling his mates. Now I work silently.

I try not to watch at night as the lights burn in the cannery. I know what they're doing. Just as Mr. Stanford Aisley predicted, our income has risen considerably. We don't need any more than we have. There is plenty for the family's education already. I've given a substantial donation to the school so that they may hire more teachers. There is a new play area with swings and games for the children. Next year there will be a music teacher in City School!

I've given enough to the hospital, in Hiram's name, that they will be able remodel and add twelve more beds. They've taken the field where we used to grow our crops and put in some of their own. Some of our old cannery employees work the fields again, this time to feed the hospital patients.

My bairn are content and live well. I've promised Sarah she'll be able to attend a college in Portland, called Reed College, when she finishes her studies here. They happily accept young women and someone as bright as Sarah will be at the top of their list, of that I'm sure.

The boys have been asking for an automobile. I know the day will come when I have to buy them one. Charles would have relished the thought of his sons traveling the countryside in the latest motorized contraption. For now, they will have to content themselves watching others drive down the new highway from our porch.

I won't allow them to set foot inside the cannery. They've asked to work in the same space as their Da, but I tell them they are meant for other things. I remind them there is plenty to do around here and at the hospital. Surely, they'll defy me soon.

There is no more space for money. Especially the money that has come from ill-gotten gains. This isn't who you taught me to be, Da. I know that. I would offer to send money over to our brothers, but I know what you'd say. "Only worthwhile when ye work for it."

I've got to come up with a solution. I wish you were here to help me sort this. I feel like an old woman, nearing forty-four. It doesn't seem age lessons a girl's need for her Da. I can fix this for myself and for Sister Faye.

Maybe I can find someone new to Aisley Lumber Township, someone who hasn't heard of Mr. Stanford Aisley yet. Someone bright-eyed and eager to build a name for themselves, as Sister Faye and I were when we arrived. Maybe we'll all move somewhere with sunshine. Even though we've lived all this time with clouds and rain, the mind always craves a bit of sunlight in the dark days of winter.

There is also one other option. At first, I didn't allow myself to think such thoughts, but the further down this dark road we travel, the more I think about it, the more it makes sense for all under this roof.

Your Devoted Dochter,
Fiona Flanagan Scheddy

Chapter Thirty-One

PINEY FALLS, OREGON

isley Lumber Township Herald
October 20ᵗʰ, 1926
Yesterday, in the bitter wind and cold of our winter days, our fair mayor declared our city would hereby be known as Flanagan. After the passing of their husbands, Charles and Albert Todd Scheddy, wives Fiona and Faye Scheddy changed their surnames to Flanagan, and with that, made their purpose in life that of charitable giving. Any number of locals remember the women's large dinners for any with an empty belly when the canning season was done. In addition to Flanagan Lane Hospital and City School, the women donate countless hours sewing clothing for those who lost their last pennies to a gambling debt. With the help of respected foremen, the women kept the business open until their deaths.

They, along with their also ill-fated husbands, moved into the cove seeing the potential for growth. The cannery grew from a few workers to over 100, helping this tiny gathering of homes to grow into a bona fide town.

Alongside the cannery, growth occurred throughout the city. A fine hotel blossomed next door, where tourists could view the operations or stroll along another board-walk to try lavender lemon or strawberry hazelnut ice cream.

They hosted weekly luncheons for the wives and monthly suppers for the entire staff, often creating their special Scottish stout stew, made from the brew produced just across the way from the cannery.

It is rumored the women took their lives because of the tension of running such a rough business without the guidance of their husbands. In the weeks preceding their deaths, Fiona Flanagan was seen about town looking sullen and withdrawn. Faye Flanagan, cheerful as always, gave away her fine china and best silver to the needy.

It was at the insistence of Widow Aisley herself that the town changed its name. "My husband respected these women as did I. He would want nothing more than to honor them. As he said many times, a woman is only as good as her name. That goes for a village as well. It's time we had a proper name for our little community and I can think of none better."

Chapter Thirty-Two

PINEY FALLS, OREGON

I'm standing in line at Cosmic Cakes and Antiquery. This Capricornus square donut-muffin-y thing has become a dangerous addiction. Well, all of his baked goods must have something addictive in them.

Spending my days in the office, I always avoided the food at breakfast meetings. I figured I would spend the rest of my day fighting food cravings, so I might as well not eat when I wasn't fully awake. No food and lattes, half foam. The old me.

Now that I'm out exploring, hiking I might be brave enough to call it, I'm ravenous most mornings. I don't know how those woodsy types stay so thin.

The smell of something new wafts up to my nostrils. "Boötes-Berry Cinnamon Scones, one of Cosmo's specialties," I hear someone in front of me say. "Wouldn't have learned my constellations without this guys' muffins."

There are five people in front of me and only three in the display case. I try not to panic.

The place is buzzing today. All six tables are full and someone has placed a few extra folding chairs around one table where a meeting appears to be taking place.

"The new lumber mill is surveying some of the forest. I know it's not a popular idea, but gosh darn it, this is fresh business. We need to take it where we can." The man with an exceptionally bushy mustache and no hair on his head takes a slurp of his coffee.

A short man wearing medical scrubs leans forward on his elbows and half-whispers, "Gary, you didn't hear? They've stopped for now. Had all of their equipment out in the woods, off Piney Falls Pathway and someone vandalized it. Looks like they took a sledgehammer to most of it. Bunch of rowdy kids, I'm sure."

I turn around and try not to stare, though they are all wearing the green nametags and as a tourist, I'm entitled to ask each of them for whatever strange thing they're hawking.

"They didn't catch anyone? They sure it was kids? Don't know many enthusiastic enough to lug a sledgehammer up that steep path." A third man with a big belly and large hands adds.

They all chuckle.

"Hard to tell who's out in them woods. You remember when they found that old-timer near five years ago? Said in the paper he'd been living off the land for nearly a decade. Forgot how to speak, he'd been alone so long."

"Sure he smelled like it." Gary comments, causing the table to erupt in laughter once more.

"Miss Anders? I can take your order."

Doris? Dana? I can't remember her name. *Welcome to Piney Falls! Ask me about seasonal taffy flavors.* She has covered the top half of her nametag with black tape.

"I'll take one of those blueberry scones," I say, staring back at the table, hoping there is more information forthcoming. Now they're discussing the fishing report.

"Sorry, Gladys Petrie from public records just called and asked if I'd save her the last one." She leans over the counter and whispers, "She's ninety-seven, so everybody just lets her have her way. She'll forget about it before she gets here, but I've got to pretend like its saved for her anyway, just in case this is a good day." She winks.

"I'll take Ursa's Major Square Donut instead. And I'll take that scone to Gladys. I'm heading there anyway."

There is nowhere to sit, so I walk to the antique room next door to the painting that caught my eye the other day. It's a watercolor of a man with large, sad eyes. He's standing in the woods, looking toward the ocean. It looks so familiar.

I walk in the other room, carrying it carefully with

my coffee and sack in the other hand. "What is this? And how much to do you want for it?"

Doris/Dana squints as she stares at the painting. "Oh, I know what this is. Painted by Fiona Scheddy. That's the rumor anyway. I've never believed it. Supposed to be her husband standing in the yard of their house, watching for her. Last I knew, Cosmo was asking twenty-five dollars for it."

"What? It was painted by the founder of the town! I'll give you two-hundred dollars."

All the noise seems to have been sucked out of the room. "You want to overpay me for that painting? Why in the world would you do that?"

"This woman was a treasure! There would be no Piney Falls without her!" I'm shouting now. Why, I'm not sure.

"Take her money, don't argue," someone snickers from one of the tables.

Doris/Dana shrugs and takes the painting from my arm. "I'll wrap it up in brown paper for ya, hon," she says. Everyone continues staring at me as I wait. *Break the tension with your smile, Marketing with Flair Seminar, 2007.* I slept with...Andy? John? I can't remember his name.

I walk over to the table where the men have grown quiet. I turn to the man in scrubs. "Maybe you haven't noticed," I bend down to see his nametag. *Ask me about a Sea Salt and Coffee Grounds Massage.* "but she put little symbols in the painting. Ron."

"Sorry, but why does that matter?" He asks.

I don't know, to be honest. I haven't quite put things together yet. "Well, Ron. It's simple. Fiona Flanagan had a purpose for everything she did. She wanted to send a message, before she jumped. A message about how important women were to this community!"

"Here's your painting, dear, enjoy." Doris/Dana arrives, as the men stare at me awkwardly. "You'll be on your way then?"

As I walk down two blocks to the public records building, there are too many thoughts swirling around in my head, from 1925 to the present. My mind quickly drifts to my life ahead.

My month-long vacation has almost ended. I have no job prospects; I haven't even tried looking. I can't bring myself to care. More concerning to me, I've tried several times to contact the owner of the home I'm staying in. All I have is an email address. When I ask about extending my stay, the response is just a series of smiley faces. Sometimes on two lines. I don't know whether to pack my bags or just plan on staying until I'm kicked out.

I walk up the steps and into the building, where I find Gladys sitting with her orthopedic shoes perched on the desk.

She looks annoyed with me. "Can I help you? Office is closed for lunch." It is 10:30.

"Gladys Petrie? I was in here the other day. I think we may have gotten off on the wrong foot. I apologize..."

"Huh?" She eyes me suspiciously. "How do you know me? Oh, nametag. I never remember this damn thing is on my chest. Washed it twice." *Welcome to Piney Falls! I'm Gladys. Ask me about our 2 beach umbrellas for rent.*

She clearly has no recollection of me. For that I'm grateful. "I'd like to search the records. Then I'd like to ask you some questions..."

"You can search. But I'm on lunch. No questions until I'm back."

"I brought your scone from Cosmo's," I add hopefully.

"Didn't order one," she sniffs, pulling her feet from the desk beside a blue typewriter. She pulls a large key ring from the desk drawer and motions for me to follow her as she shuffles to a large, wooden door. I stand, waiting for her to unlock it. Instead she shakes her head.

"Is this the room? I'd like to look..."

"You need keys. Thought you'd just ask for them. Outsiders can be a little dense." She drops the keyring and I barely catch it.

"Bring 'em back to the desk when you're done." She turns and shuffles away.

The door opens to a magical place that looks like it's been untouched for decades. I decide to search records for a lot of things. I don't think I'm supposed to have access to everything in this room, but I'm not going to point that out. I'm also not going to ask if these things are available online. I peek my head out and am relieved when I see her sitting at her desk removing the scone from its bag, in another world.

There is a lengthy file for death certificates. I find the one for Zion Scheddy. For some reason, the autopsy report is clipped to it. I don't see that on any other death certificates.

It lists the cause of death as "drowning." There are several descriptive words about the wound to the face, blunt force trauma, and then distinctive marks on the body. I see something at the bottom that almost seems aimed at me. *Please read carefully!*

Gladys shuffles back and forth in front of the room. I think she may be watching me out of the corner of her eye but I can't be sure. I can't pull out my phone and take a picture without it being obvious. It's as quiet as a morgue in here.

Not that I've been an angel my entire life, but as a whole I'm opposed to stealing. Is it a felony to steal a death certificate? If I'm planning to bring it back? I ponder that for a minute. The centenarian sneezes, causing her entire body to shudder. She has to grasp the nearest thing to her, which is a desk that is partially obscured by the door to this room.

I slip the death certificate into my pants. When you're panicking, you do strange things. I look up to see Gladys standing in the doorway.

"Are you done with lunch?"

She pulls a bony wrist close to her eyes and studies her watch. "Could be." She doesn't appear to have noticed my theft.

"I'm assuming you've been here a long time, Gladys. Do you have memories of what happened when Fallen Branch fell apart?"

"Some, I'd say. What do you want to know?"

"What do you remember about the murder? About the trial?"

"Don't recall any trial. The young feller turned himself in. That was the end of that. Those freaks thought they'd have the run of the town after that. We made sure they didn't. Hired a fancy private eye to keep track of them just to make sure they wouldn't cause trouble. Kept a list here at the courthouse so's we'd know who they were."

"Do you have that list? Could I just peek at it?"

She moves at a snail's pace to the very back of the room, on the furthest rack of books. She pulls a large file out and hands it to me. "Should be up-to-date. Least up to 2005. It's as complete as we could make it. Some of those kooks changed their names more than once."

"Thank you, Gladys!"

I spend the next two days making calls, confirming what I already suspected. I have everything I need to write my story. Whichever story I choose to tell. I hope I'm able to tell the right people without too much pain.

Chapter Thirty-Three

AISLEY LUMBER TOWNSHIP, OREGON

Dearest Da,

Today I awoke with lightness in my heart and finally, a plan to fix our problems. I baked a batch of huckleberry muffins and walked over to the Aisley home, after I knew Mr. Stanford Aisley would be gone for the day.

Mrs. Aisley is a lonely woman, I think. She finds most in Aisley Lumber Township to be beneath her and that leaves her very much to herself. She'll jabber on to her maid about the doings of her next-door neighbor and the latest people to disappear from her husband's employ. When they might shop at the store together, she doesn't acknowledge the poor woman exists. I finally realized the reason she looks forward to her time in San Francisco is less about society and more about her time away from her husband. He encouraged her to move there permanently but for some reason she refuses. Now she spends all of her days closed up in her home, pestering her maid.

Mrs. Aisley was surprised to see me. That morning, as we brunched on my huckleberry muffins and a smooth Earl Grey tea, she told me of her plans for an extended trip to Europe. "You should come, Fi!" She touched my arm as if we were close confidantes. I thought about a trip with her. Hours of tedious dress shopping and being seen in the stuffiest pretentious clubs. After I'd spent my entire adult life amongst those with no means, who were twice as interesting.

"Thank you, but I have something of utmost importance to discuss with you," I said, careful not to stare her in the eye.

She leaned forward, excited to be needed. "What can I do, dearie?"

I reminded her of the story of Lachlan Douglas, how I thought he would be 'shanghaied,' as they say when someone is kidnapped to spend a year's servitude on a ship. I knew she already had an idea that her husband was selling drugs from our building, but I needed to be honest. That's what you've always said, right, Da?

"Perhaps you can help me, Mrs. Aisley," I continued cautiously. "As you can well imagine, I don't want my sons to grow up as dealers of drugs to the far east. I need to remove our names from the building and extract us from this situation."

Her demeanor instantly changed, from sweet, innocent mouse to aggressive, long-chinned rat with beady, evil eyes. "You came to me for help and I've helped you. More than you could have ever expected, really. Got rid of that horrible Mr. Douglas. My husband isn't one to listen to my concerns. The fact that he was willing to help you at all, well, that is quite remarkable, don't you think?"

He made a wonderful business for himself out of my blackmail, I thought. I didn't say anything though. It was best to keep that to myself.

"Don't you think I know what goes on? The things he does in the name of business? It's those unpleasantries that kept me and our Ophelia in niceties, just as your husband did for you."

I wasn't sure I heard her correctly. "My husband was a wanderer, but he was an honest wanderer. Never involving himself in the dark dealings of Mr. Stanford Aisley." I hoped she hadn't learned of Albert Todd's infatuation with the brothel. Of course, she had. She knew everything about everyone in this town, dead or alive.

She laughed, causing me to feel anger rising from my stomach, wanting to lurch out and seize her by the spindly little neck.

"Oh, my dear. I thought you knew. Your coming here the first day of your arrival in town wasn't by accident. Charles and Albert Todd, rest their souls, contacted my Stanford while you were still in New York. They wanted to start their cannery in order to sell their drugs. They were world travelers, indeed. But those travels were to buy and sell the best opium. The finest heroin. They were in Scotland selling ecgonine when they met you and your sister."

I try to keep my face straight, without emotion.

"Mr. Aisley met them in New York several times and gave them the money needed to start their business. You didn't think they were enterprising enough to start this business all on their own? There was no bank loan. They were just simple men with big dreams."

All of the time our husbands spent away from us over the years, we'd just assumed they were experiencing new places purely for enjoyment. "No," I replied. "That can't be. I did the bookwork for our business. I knew where every penny was spent."

"Fiona, you are a naïve woman. You only know where the cannery money was spent. Albert had a special safe. I'm sure you remember the hole in the floor you found after your husband's death? Mr. Aisley's men came and removed the safe."

I was stunned, Da. I couldn't believe our boys had fooled us all along. All of those happy trips around the country. "Am I to believe they took these trips for Mr. Aisley?"

Mrs. Aisley went to the kitchen and whispered in the ear of her downstairs made. In a few minutes, the woman returned with photographs. She handed them to me without comment.

To my shock and horror, there were Albert Todd and Charles in front of a barber shop, a laundry and a large restaurant. They had their arms around the owners in a jovial manner. "What are these?"

"Businesses your husband and brother-in-law opened over the years for my husband. Thanks to them, Mr. Aisley has operations in ten states. All selling some type of...medication." She smiled. "The lumber industry made us prosperous, but your boys helped to ensure we'll never be without comfort. The money you've been making is what your husbands already had acquired. Unfortunately, before their deaths they spent their added wealth on their travels and...extra activities. I'm sorry they didn't properly care for their families."

All of the anguish suffered by our combined families, the abuse of Lachlan Douglas, all endured to keep a business running that wasn't really a business at all.

"Why wouldn't he just buy the building from us, or take it? Why involve two lonely widows in his criminal activities? How could you let him treat us so poorly?" I couldn't hide my anger.

"It's better to have the business in your name. The authorities have recently been interested in what may or may not be coming into the ports. With your name on those cans of salmon, they won't worry. Two widows running a business isn't cause for alarm."

Tears streamed down my cheeks. I'm not one for showing emotion publicly, as you well remember, Da. "You won't help then?" I finally asked helplessly.

She sighed a make-believe sign of distress that brought her maid running. "Nothing dearie," she said sweetly before returning her gaze to me. "There's nothing I can do, nor would I if I could. But you, dear, always have options. You'll do what's best, of that I'm sure." She showed me to the door and closed it before I had a chance to respond. I didn't need anything else from this lecherous woman anyway.

I couldn't imagine what options might be available to me. This man had control of our business and who knows how many others. His name was on the town. He had been pulling the strings in both Scheddy families ever since we married.

I began to think about two adventuring brothers, ending up in the Scottish countryside looking for brides. I never questioned their wandering nature before. It made them exciting. Now I could see their travels were only possible because of Mr. Stanford Aisley. We were but one more product of his business dealings.

I found Faye sitting in the kitchen, staring into nothingness. I asked if she might accompany me on a walk to the falls. Though we walked in silence, I took her hand. We still had our sisterly bond and that was stronger than any bad words that had been thrown between us.

When we arrived at the top of Piney Falls, we laid back on the biggest rock, drinking in the mist from the falls. Our minds calmed as they always did when we reached this most perfect area. It was the one place over the years where we could always count on finding clarity. "I'm going to tell you a story, Faye. You might not understand, but I don't have anyone else I can share this burden with." I proceeded to tell her the entire sordid tale, not worrying about her gentle state of mind. I let go the story of Albert Todd's other wife and our husband's illegal dealings.

When I finished, I sat up and stared at Sister Faye. Her eyes were the same, dull and lifeless orbs they had been off and on for three years. I closed my eyes and wondered what would happen next.

"You've had this burden too long, Sister," she remarked. I looked at her in shock. "I know how to make things right for everyone."

I'll finish this story in the next letter. I've much to attend to now.

Your Devoted Dochter,
Fiona Flanagan Scheddy

Chapter Thirty-Four

AISLEY LUMBER TOWNSHIP, OREGON

Dearest Da,

To my complete astonishment, Faye heard every single word I uttered. Somewhere in that addled, scarred mind, a real person still existed. She barely breathed but the fire was still burning. And even more unbelievably, she had well-thought-out ideas on how to proceed. At first, I objected to her extreme plan of action, but I saw that she was right, we had reached the end of our options.

We've lived a wonderful life here. Beginning our time with nothing and making two fine homes, raising beautiful bairn and starting a hospital. There's nothing to feel bad about when it comes to what we've accomplished. It's what we've left undone that bothers me.

We spent the next three weeks in preparation. Saying goodbye to employees we came to love and cherish. Mr. Samuel Li, who visited us often to bring fine tea from China, suspected we had made a decision regarding our future.

"You've unpacked the bag I gave you and don't like what you've found," he remarked.

"There is no way to change its contents," I replied grimly.

He nodded. "Leave no ends untied then."

I painted a picture of the view from Scheddy Manor. The rolling waves and the light blue sky that meets it on the days we're lucky enough to be rid of the infernal clouds. The teachers at City School were happy to display it. Maybe they'll remember me for a time.

I'll say that I regret never seeing Scotland again. Rolling hills and green pasture land like no other. It's too bad my bairn will never enjoy a frolic through the pasture of Flanagan Farm.

After all was prepared, I felt better about our plans. All would work out as it should. We packed up all the bairns, telling them we would join them soon. I rented a house for them close to Sarah's new college. The lady who owned it was a widow whose own children were grown and moved. We spoke on the telephone twice. Da, you wouldn't believe those things. It's like having a person right there. It'll change the world, I daresay. When Charles insisted we buy one, I thought it silly. Then he used it to phone Albert Todd, just across the road. The weather was poor and he didn't want to put on boots and the collection of rain clothes we normally wear. I saw the value in that. No use getting wet when we didn't need to do it.

I spoke to Widow Peakman and she assured me the bairns would be in good hands until our supposed arrival. She'd give them chores as I'd asked, since we know that idle hands never produce good things. She looked forward to our meeting. I didn't comment as I knew that day would never come. She also looked forward to the life five new bodies would bring into her home.

They were excited for their new lives in Portland as well. Sarah, especially. Faye told her boys they would find new wonders and not to be afraid to try each and every one. "Aren't you going to join us on all of our adventures?" Padrug asked. Faye smiled and rubbed his head. "You're old enough tae see the adventures on your own. You don't want your mam there making a fuss."

That seemed to satisfy him. I was glad my boys didn't ask the same. The night before they left, I tucked extra money into each of their traveling bags. I told Sarah to make sure they didn't spend it before they were settled.

"Though it may be some time before we get the cannery sold. I'd like you to watch your brothers and your cousins, as you always do. You're always far more grown up than the rest of us." I winked at my dochter.

"Mam, I know you aren't coming with us," Sarah said that night. Always the smart one. I never could lie to her. But I couldn't tell her what we were planning. She needed to remember me as a loving mam, someone who only wanted the best for her.

"Not to worry. You'll be seeing me again, that I promise you." I kissed her soft cheek and held her hand until she was comforted. "You need to remember to care for yourself." She started to protest, but I put a finger to her lips. "Care for yourself. That means you find the courses in your schooling that lead you to whatever you want to become. Your Nana wanted strang women in her line. I can't think of a better example. Make no mind what others tell you of your future. You're a Flanagan woman, through and through. Understand?"

She nodded her head, though I could still see uncertainty in her eyes. We hugged, holding each other tightly. No matter how I consoled her, she knew the truth of it.

The next day we saw them off. Faye patted her bairn on the heads as if they were heading to a day of school and not a brand-new life in Portland. She didn't shed one tear. She appeared gleeful over our decision. It made me cold inside to think of her unable to feel emotion, but maybe that was better for what lay ahead.

Lachlan Douglas had a gun that he kept on the top shelf of Faye's closet. He got it down several times to threaten the boys when they were unruly. The first time I saw him do this was the night after our Fourth of July celebration.

Mr. Stanford Aisley always put on a good show. Each year he paid a fancy marching band to come in from Astoria. They wore bright costumes and had big plumes in their hats. We'd never heard such delightful sounds before that first year. All the women who lived here, at the time, only thirty or so, made pies for a pie eating contest.

After dark, there were fireworks filling up the night sky. Mr. Stanford Aisley gave everyone the day off from work and made quite a spectacle of himself. Even gave a speech about his good deeds in the community. Charles always said to smile and pretend like we believed the silliness coming out of his mouth. Mrs. Aisley, always wearing colorful dresses from Paris and carrying a matching parasol, sat on the stage beside him. Oh yes, Da, he had a stage built every year. Mostly so he would have a place to perch his tiny body and look tall. And then he could do his blustering atop a large crate, specially painted to say, "Mr. Stanford Aisley, Town Leader." The story was that he had it made so that the pie eaters could be seen by everyone. We knew better.

And Mrs. Aisley, she put on a show to equal her husband's. After the first year, when I realized how much she despised him, I began to notice the acting she did whenever he was around. Batting her eyes and tilting her head towards him. He knew she wasn't in love with him, and by the words of our employees, he spent his fair share of time in the brothels so he wasn't in love with her either.

I saw her clutch her hands together tightly, until they turned white, when he would talk about his success.

That Fourth of July, Lachlan Douglas had been testing the alcohol made by the Norwegian men. Aquavit. The same thing they used as a remedy for the Spanish Flu. So strang it would remove the barnacles from the boats, I remember Charles saying. Lachlan Douglas stumbled up our path at half past midnight. Faye, as always, sat in the kitchen, drinking tea and waiting for him.

I heard yelling and ran down to see what was happening. One of the boys left a toy car in the kitchen and he slipped on it. When he got up, he hit Faye so hard she fell against the hot stove, burning her arm.

By now the whole house was awake, including the offending boy. He pushed Lachlan Douglas away and helped his mother to her feet. Usually Lachlan Douglas would box the boys' ears if they bothered him. But on this night, he went to the bedroom and returned soon after with his gun. He took the boy by his collar and held him up, pointing the gun at his brow. All of us, the boys, Sarah and I begged him to put it away. "Faye can't lose another child," I begged.

For some reason, that made him drop the boy. He turned and went upstairs to his bedroom without saying another word. The rest of us huddled in the kitchen, crying over what we had just seen. I wished that one incident would have been enough for Faye to tell him to leave. I don't know why it wasn't. Now, years later, Lachlan Douglas's destruction of choice would be used to protect our family.

I looked around the house thinking of all of the wonderful memories our little family shared. Each bairn's birth, the sounds of tiny squeaks of life all hours of the night and day. Charles marking their growth on the wall by notching it out next to each name, talking excitedly about our days.

The lemony smell of fresh Tantallion cakes in the oven after a long day in the cannery. My feet ached as I worked the shortbread dough, but I knew the bairns' faces would crinkle with delight when they saw their favorite the next morning. Charles would spread my marionberry jam on top of them. I thought about you, how your merry green eyes would roll in disgust of such a doing. The bairns took up the practice as well, and for all the years after, no one would eat my cakes unless there was a jar of jam in the pantry. I panicked for moment, wondering if I'd tucked that recipe into Sarah's bag. I had.

Sitting on the porch together after a long day of labor, working our garden together and bringing baskets of vegetables to the hospital. We laughed as the boys re-enacted a movie they'd seen at the new cinema house. As Sister Faye and I nursed our tired bodies, we marveled at the energy they possessed.

So many happy memories. Now it was time for another family to make their own. Maybe someday they would come to learn about the two Flanagan sisters who gave everything they had to become successful women in a small American town.

Your Devoted Dochter,
Fiona Flanagan Scheddy

Chapter Thirty-Five

PINEY FALLS, OREGON

When I call Cosmo to ask him to hike to the top of Piney Falls with me, he sounds shocked. "Are you sure? I thought you weren't ready to tackle that monster yet?"

"I've been hiking every day for three weeks." The words I never thought would leave my lips. "I think I can handle it. I have something really important I need to talk to you about." I hope he won't note the anxiety in my voice.

When he arrives at my door, he hugs me warmly. He smells of cinnamon and cloves. That mixed with the glorious forest smell makes me happy. Yes, those smells are now happy smells in my life. Before, I would have considered them the scent of the mall candle store dweller.

"Just go slow," I warn. "I may be persistent, but I'm not fast."

"Okay," he chuckles. "Fair enough."

He hands me a bag and it feels warm on the bottom.

"Libra-lly Lemon Curd and Boötes-Berry Cinnamon Scones, I heard there was a run on them the other day and a beautiful woman left empty-handed."

I chuckle. "She didn't exactly leave empty-handed. She's been consuming plenty of your baked goods. But thank you. I'll enjoy these."

I lock the door and turn to leave. "Do you know who owns this place? I've been trying to get ahold of my landlord for a couple of weeks now. All I get are smiley faces."

"No, I don't, but it sounds like a six-year-old owns your house. I used to know everyone on this road. Once I got out of prison, the second prison of my life, I came out here frequently. Just proving to myself that I could without anyone's permission."

"What a life you've had," I remark.

"Those memories are so deeply ingrained; every time I made it to the top, I felt like Zion was right there watching me. I've never been able to shake that feeling. Guess that's why they say these kinds of scars are for life."

"I wish I could help you. You've gone through so much."

He touches my shoulder. It causes an electricity throughout my entire body.

We start out at his pace and then I grab his arm. "This might take longer than you anticipated."

"You know, when I was allowed my once-a-year

visit to the top of Piney Falls, I always confessed my misdeeds to the Flanagan sisters. I knew it really made Zion angry. He usually stopped me about halfway through, told me I didn't know what I was talking about and I'd better go back and meditate for a few days. That meant sitting in a tent by myself. He didn't realize that much time away from him was heaven."

"What a great guy," I say sarcastically. "I don't understand why women who died so long ago would upset him so much."

"Nothing about this town made him happy. He stood back in the bushes, watching and listening to whatever you said. He really expected something profound to come out of your mouth, or at least a confession to a crime that interested him. He said he couldn't hear, but I think he was lying."

"I have no doubt." I'm taking baby steps, hoping I won't become breathless before we reach the top. I don't want him to think I can't do this.

"One of my friends came up here and confessed he stole some bread. After that, he wasn't allowed to eat bread."

Cosmo continues telling me stories of cult members and their punishments for seemingly insignificant crimes. I can't believe how many people were punished for so little.

"Cosmo, do you know what happened to the children of Faye and Fiona? They seem to have disappeared as far as I can tell historically."

"The daughter, Sarah. I know she was a doctor

somewhere around Portland. One of the first women in the state. Probably can't find her because she went by the name Sarah Flanagan. She didn't care about anyone's ability to pay. Later in life, she became a researcher. Loved doing those autopsies."

"And the boys?"

"At least one of Faye's children had some problems with the law. The oldest boy, Percival I think, ended up in prison for murder. I heard rumors the other one, Padrug, was institutionalized. Fiona's boys were successful bankers. I have no proof, really. That's the coffee shop gossip."

Everything is fitting together exactly as I thought it would.

40 minutes goes by quickly and I see the sign, "Piney Falls," next to a railing. I'm barely sweating. Not the Lanie Anders who arrived a month ago.

I gaze at the falls in wonder. It is a four-tiered-display that plunges into a deep, aqua-blue pool. At the base it is foamed into a lather that looks like a luxurious bubble bath. As I begin to get closer, the noise increases; growling and rumbling. It is energetic, magnificent and terrifying given its history of claiming so many former members of Fallen Branch. It is much louder than the Little Cone, forcing its audience into quiet submission. I have to stand for a moment in awe.

Cosmo takes my arm and guides me over to a flat rock. "Breathtaking, isn't it?"

I nod. "I can see why people need to come here to confess their sins. No one can hear what they're saying," I chuckle. We sit, feeling the spray on our sweaty faces.

He leans over and kisses me gently on the cheek. Feelings well up inside me and I push them back down. After he put his head on my lap the other day, I shouldn't be surprised, but I am. I would never allow a man to do that. At least a man who wasn't Cosmo Hill.

"I hope that was okay," he says timidly. "Something came over me. That can happen at this particular location where there's always too much emotion."

"You bring women up here routinely to kiss them?" I joke, remembering what Cedar told me about his lack of dating history.

He blushes. "No, I meant people come here to confess their bad deeds and sometimes just to let their true selves come through. I guess I'm finally feeling like I can do that with you. Now that you're leaving." He looks at the ground. "Guys in prison used to talk about their women back home. I thought they were weak. Fallen Branch taught us relationships were for those who didn't have vision for themselves. So, I sat alone in that cell, waiting for something miraculous to happen. Isn't that crazy?"

"Not at all. I did the opposite, thinking I was making progress of my own."

"I felt something that first day. I think you felt it too." Cosmo puts his arm on my shoulder.

I nod weakly. "Cos, I'm kind of a mess. I'm not sure..."

He puts his lips up to my ear. "Maybe I should try again? Just to make sure we both feel it's done right?"

Cosmo leans in but I put my finger on his chin. "As much as I would enjoy that, I wanted you to come up here with me so I could ask you about something delicate. It is the place of truth, right?"

He nods. "You're scaring me, Lanie."

I ignore his comment. "Can you tell me about the night you... What happened with Zion?"

He sits upright. "That's why we're here? I thought you wanted to spend time with me because you couldn't resist my baker-man sexiness." He chuckles. "Okay, I suppose you deserve that."

I take his hand. "I won't judge you. He was a monster."

He lets out a big long sigh. "Here goes. There was a big city council meeting that night. Cedar worked for weeks making slides, putting together facts and creating this big—"

"Marketing package. I've had lots of experience." I break in. "That's what I did for a living." *Did?*

"Yeah, that sounds right. She put in all of her non-commune-regulated hours doing that for him. I was starting to wonder if something funny was going on. Women who spent time with him were usually involved with him in some way, and Cedar was with him night and day. She'd get back to our barrack and roll out her mat after midnight every night. She promised me it was all about this presentation.

She was so proud of herself. Made me promise I'd

come and watch her. She was nineteen going on thirty; such confidence in that kid. That's the good thing about cult life, we learned to be self-sufficient early on."

He leans back and locks his hands around his knee. "She spoke for about thirty minutes. The whole room was so quiet you could hear a pin drop. When she finished the presentation, I saw Zion wink at her. It infuriated me. I thought maybe she had been lying to me, that they really did have some kind of inappropriate relationship going on.

"A guy from the city began explaining why it wouldn't be a good idea to make this a manufacturing hub, at least using Zion's ideas. How crazy the rest of the world would find it to buy their gym clothes from a cult. He didn't want the city to become Fallen Branch, with good reason." He stops for a minute, lost in thoughts of his former life. I can see pain in his eyes. I grab his hand.

"Cedar watched Zion, waiting for him to stand up and defend her hard work. Instead, the bastard stood up and laughed. He told them he made a mistake putting a child in charge of such an important project. He would submit a new proposal for more realistic ways he could run businesses in town and bring in more people.

"Poor Sis. She was humiliated. But in true Fallen Branch fashion, she sat there until the end of the meeting. Don't leave a gathering until Zion dismisses you. He waved his back row of identical men in identical beards out the door. Finally, he dismissed Cedar. She ran out of that place and even though I was still supposed to wait for approval, I ran after her."

"Did you find her?"

"Not for a long time. I thought she might have taken the short cut home, so I went down that path first. When I got back to the main road, I saw her running away. There behind her was what I thought was a dead animal in the road. We didn't waste anything, so I was going to drag it back to camp. When I got up close, I saw it was Zion."

"He was already dead?"

"I'd never seen a dead body before. We killed wild animals for food, but when people died, they were 're-purposed.' That meant burnt on a funeral pyre and their ashes spread on our garden. You had to be assigned to that job and I hadn't." He looks at me uncomfortably. "Sorry, that can be hard to hear, if you're not from our group."

I shrug. After being in Piney Falls for several weeks, none of this is shocking.

"I got up close and saw this horribly mangled face. If I hadn't seen the medallion, I wouldn't have known who it was."

I nod. All of my suspicions are being confirmed.

"There was a heavy branch, bloodied, laying nearby. I realized immediately what happened. Cedar was waiting for him to walk down the path and she took out years of frustration.

"I drug his body up here, to the top of the falls and

pushed it off. The next morning, I went in to the police station and told them I killed him. I didn't want my sister to pay for something I should have done years earlier."

"That was so noble. Not a lot of nineteen-year-olds would have that much presence of mind." I hope he knows I'm being sincere. "And you never spoke about this with Cedar?"

"I was in jail until I went to prison. Nobody would dare bail me out, even though most of them felt exactly the same about him. What if Zion came back in some form and punished them? Didn't talk to Cedar or anyone else."

I think hard for a moment. I need to share this with him, no matter how difficult it will be. "Have you ever had a conversation with Cedar about it?"

"No, it's too painful for both of us. We didn't even talk about it when I was in prison. After I got out, I just wanted to move on."

"Cos, what if I told you I didn't think Cedar killed Zion? She told me the story of finding the body and thinking you did it."

His beautiful eyes widen. "What? Maybe she's confused. It was very traumatizing for her that night."

"I read the police report. All it says is that you confessed. Cedar came in and told them you were innocent. They asked why she knew and she said everyone had a motive. They examined her at that time for signs of a struggle. That branch used as the murder weapon was pretty heavy. Much too heavy for a little person like Cedar to continually beat on someone without some kind of marks on her, cuts or something. That was the end of the story, as far as they were concerned. Loving sister trying to protect her brother."

"I didn't know that. Makes me love her even more." Cosmo squeezes my hand. "The public defender I had wasn't real interested in helping me. He didn't want this to bring bad publicity to a town that was trying to distance itself from a cult. As far he was concerned, the quicker I was locked up, the sooner everybody could move on."

We sit in silence for a minute, listening to the rushing water.

He turns to face me. "The way you said all of that, you must have some theory. Who did it then? Someone on the city council, or someone else at Fallen Branch? So many people hated him."

"What if no one killed him?"

"Lanie, I drug that heavy body myself up to these falls. I'm not real educated, but I know someone died."

"Someone. But not necessarily Zion. I've been taking lots of walks by myself out here in the woods. I've found some interesting things. I've seen some medallions. Vem told me you all had individual medallions made. I think it's the one Zion wore."

Cosmo leans back on his elbows. "Now I know that can't be true. It was around his neck when he went over. There were several made similar to his, you know, people who thought they were on his level. This guy named Hawk..."

"You told me that his face was unrecognizable when you found him. What if it were someone else who died?"

"That's just crazy. After that night, there was no more Zion. The cult disbanded."

"While I was researching the Flanagan sisters, I looked into other things. Cedar has a list of former Fallen Branch members. So does Gladys, but hers is outdated, no surprise there. The city council asked Cedar to compile one so they could keep an eye on them in case anyone decides they want to start causing trouble. I contacted all of them. Cos, there's only one person I couldn't find on either list."

I want to stand, move around, be in control. There is no way though. I feel helpless, delivering information that will destroy the most magnificent man I've ever met. "Cos, I need to tell you that I spoke to your mother. The woman you thought was your mother. I couldn't find the other woman."

"She's still alive? I bet those two don't even remember the names of their kids."

"She feels bad. Maybe. I couldn't tell for sure. But the most interesting thing she told me is that she left Fallen Branch before your trial. By herself."

"Where's dad? Did he run off with someone?"

"There's no record of your father after Fallen Branch. Ever."

Cosmo stands up and puts his hands in his pockets. He rocks back and forth on his feet. "If my father never left the camp then another cult member did something to him. Did Zion have him locked away somewhere? Or did...Lanie, are you saying what I think you're saying?"

"I think instead of Zion dying that night, it was your father. You said yourself he was at the city council meeting."

"But... that's not possible. I know it was Zion I drug up the road. It took me three hours. Thankfully, I was in good shape then."

"You told me one of the first times I met you that all of the men were supposed to look identical to Zion." I pull the one thing I've been dreading to share the most out of my pocket. "And I found this one day. Vem told me she'd seen it here before."

"What are you doing with the medallion?" He

looks at me suspiciously. "What kind of game is this to you, Lanie?"

I stand, less-nimbly than him. "Remember, I told you I found this the other day? There's no game. I'm here to help. What I'm thinking...what I'm really thinking...is that Zion is still here, out in the woods somewhere."

"Okay, Lanie, I've totally misjudged you. I think you may need some psychological help. There's no way a person could stay hidden for over twenty years."

He is walking back and forth, back and forth. I wait until he gets close and grab his arm. "Let's look at this logically. He has survival skills. He built Fallen Branch and taught everyone to live off the land. He was a man of, let's call it pride, who didn't like to be humiliated. He found the city council meeting a very humiliating experience. Maybe he just decided the best way to end it all was to remove himself from the situation and start over."

He furrows his brows. "Okay, but why wouldn't he want to have some kind of connection with the members he liked? If he knew Cedar was his daughter, why didn't he contact her?"

"I can't answer that, but someone can. We need to search these woods. Someone, somewhere has to know."

Chapter Thirty-Seven

PINEY FALLS, OREGON

I check my messages and find none from my landlord. I'm officially a squatter. I pack my suitcase and put it in my car, just in case I come home and the locks have been changed. I have no plans for what I'll do next, after today. Lanie Anders, queen of the orderly life, has become a nomad.

Cosmo knocks on my door as I'm collecting the last few things that matter to me. After losing everything in the fire, I've developed a strong attachment to strange things, like eye shadow and socks. I pull on the fleece coat with Welcome to Piney Falls stitched on the front. I'm taking this with me. Let this mysterious landlord fine me.

"You're looking radiant," he comments as I pull my new backpack over my shoulders. The things he says would sound so transparently creepy coming out of someone else's mouth. It doesn't take much to flatter me, apparently. Every time I see him it feels like it's brand new.

"Thanks, Cos."

"I still can't believe you figured all of this stuff out. The more I thought about it last night, the more it made sense. Zion would be the type to run off and leave everyone who had become completely dependent on him. He was...is...pure evil."

I hear a dog barking and I see a white pickup parked in the driveway. There is a large, excited dog sitting in the passenger side. "Do you know whose truck this is?"

"That's me. I borrowed my buddy's truck, and his dog. His name is Muenster, after the cheese. We weren't allowed to eat cheese at Fallen Branch so when we were introduced to it, some of us went crazier than others. Me, I went for the sugar."

"Okay, I still don't understand why Muenster is here." The mustard-colored Labrador is more energy than I want on a hike.

"He's been trained as a tracking dog. He's been used to look for missing kids and hikers."

"What a great idea! I still have the medallion, maybe he can get something off of that."

"We'll have to be quick. Muenster gets excited when he finds a scent. If the chase is too fast for you, I'll go after him and you can catch up."

"Cosmo, I need to tell you something. I'm thinking about staying a little longer. This place has... I've kind of grown attached."

He smiles the broad, beautiful smile that drew me in the first time I met him. I'd like to bask in it for hours. "Is there a specific reason you're staying? Is your attachment strictly to my baking skills?"

"I have feelings for you," I blurt. Not the Lanie Anders from Chicago. A vulnerable me, looking to build something new. "I don't know how to do this, but I'm willing to try."

"I'm glad you brought that up. Lanie, I don't know how these things work either, but I'd really like... well, I'd like to date you properly. Is there some kind of process to this?"

I guffaw, not purposely to hurt his feelings. Its the absurdity of two people getting to this stage of life without an understanding of the simple dating process. "I'd like that. A lot. We'll have to take things slow, just so neither one of us feels uncomfortable."

He nods solemnly. "We'll take things your speed. I don't want to scare you away."

"Two slow-moving dinosaurs, trying to figure things out." He steps closer, putting his mouth to my ear. "I'll happily be your guinea pig." He takes my face in his soft hands and kisses me deeply. As much as I don't want it to stop, I know this has to wait.

I pull my head away and look at my watch. "We'd better start. Did I mention I'm also quite slow on the hiking trail?" There's so much I need to tell him, about my many one-night conquests, about the broken pieces of me from my childhood that still haven't been glued back together. But not right now.

We walk into the woods a bit before Cosmo takes the medal from me and puts it in front of Muenster's nose. He unhooks the leash. "Go!" he commands. Muenster lumbers off, excitedly sniffing the ground as he goes.

We walk briskly until we hear Muenster barking. "Stay with him!" I say, though not out of breath. "I'll catch up."

Muenster and I walk by ourselves for twenty minutes. I hope I didn't take a wrong turn. I don't panic, these woods are my friends now. Piney Falls might not be a bad place to settle down. Maybe I could find a place to rent for a while. I've got plenty of money saved. When we get back, I'll call Cedar and ask for realtor recommendations.

Finally, I reach a clearing and I see Cosmo and Muenster in the distance. I wave my arms wildly, hoping they'll wait. Vem's crazy gesturing has worn off on me. Cosmo waves back. It's another ten minutes before I reach them. Muenster is leashed by Cosmo's side, sitting obediently. There is no pathway covered in pine needles, as I'm used to. Just tall grass and who-knows-what lurking underneath, like my walk with Vem to the Flanagan home. I try not to think about things popping out and biting me.

"Thanks for waiting! What did he find?" Cosmo puts his hand over my mouth and points. In the distance, I see a small cabin with smoke coming out of the chimney.

"You wait here with Muenster," he whispers. "I'm

going to go up to the door and see who it is." His voice tickles my ear and makes me feel inappropriately tingly.

I nod and take the leash. I watch Cosmo walk across the empty field to the small cabin. He knocks on the door and a tall figure opens it and invites him in.

I sit patiently, realizing it is the perfect opportunity to "center myself," as Vem says.

"Staying here is the right thing," I begin, out loud. "I've made progress; no more sleeping my way to the top. I can offer to help the city market this town as a vacation resort, help fix up Flanagan Lane Hospital for tours, I could really do some good."

I gaze into Muenster's brown eyes. "Or, I could go back to Chicago. Get my house started. Find a killer job. With the resume I have, I could make twice what they were paying me at Work Ahead Office Supplies - The Most Profitable Office Supply Chain in the World. That's what a rational person would do. It makes the most sense."

Muenster lays his head on his large paws, clearly tired of my rambling. "Life was so boring when I was rational. Everything was planned. Everything was meaningless. There's something about this place – and there's definitely something about Cosmo Hill." He stares at me blankly.

I look at my watch and realize thirty minutes have passed. I wonder if tracking dogs double as attack animals? I look back at him wagging his tail, one ear flopped forward. Nope, don't think so.

"C'mon boy," I say, giving his leash a tug. I don't know how dogs work but I assume he will follow me. Instead, he seems to lead me, much faster than I am comfortable. By the time we reach the cabin, I'm completely out of breath.

The door is ajar and I can hear Cosmo's agitated voice. "What you're saying doesn't even make sense. You had everything you wanted. Why would you give it up to live like a hermit?"

I peek inside, viewing an elderly, well-built man with a grey beard that almost reaches his waist. His eyebrows are bushy and dark, in stark contrast to the gray hair covering the rest of him.

"Brother Cosmo, I've been able to continue my work out here without the constraints of society." His voice is deep and lilting. I can see why people were mesmerized by it.

"Don't call me that. That's the line of bull you were giving us at the cult camp. How is this different? And why did you abandon your daughter?"

"They were all my daughters. It was time for me to move to a higher plane. They received all the information they could from me. They needed to go out in the world and share it with everyone else. Why don't you sit down, Brother Cosmo?"

Don't do it, Cos. You need to stand tall.

"That's bullshit. Plain and simple. The night of the city council meeting, you just decided that was the time to walk away? Without telling anyone?"

"It was the best time. I could see they wouldn't

allow me to move forward. I had to change the world in a quieter way."

I can't take this any longer. I burst through the door. "You killed Cosmo's father, didn't you? To make your escape? And maybe these people who have been committing suicide were just there to speak their truth and you helped them over."

Zion looks up at me with surprise and then an eerie smile spreads over his face. "I've been watching you. You stumbled through the woods like a newborn doe. Then you grew your antlers. You're proud and sure."

"Don't try your poetic weeds on her. She's too smart to fall for it." Cosmo is irritated, but I don't want him to blow our only chance for information.

"I can handle myself," I retort. "So, you've been watching me, Zion. You know I've found all of your clues. Your real medallion, and the others you set in the corners of Fiona's house. Thinking they were like breadcrumbs to draw me to you."

"Sister November almost ruined it. I'm glad you were persistent."

"There must be a reason you wanted me to find it. And you. I also found your cheaply done medallions at the site of the old Flanagan home. Same symbols Fiona Flanagan put in the corners of her painting. Now you can tell me your story."

I sit down on a hand-carved wooden chair, completely calm, maybe out of adrenaline overload.

I'm so going to eat every one of those blueberry scones when I get home.

"You want to understand Zion?"

"Oh, here we go...we only have a few hours of daylight. We're not going to listen to the whole 'fix the world' speech. I've given her the highlights. Or let's call them low lights." Cosmo paces the room.

"It's okay, Cos. I want to hear about your father. You can tell us, right Zion? There was a reason he had to die." I remember the tough-to-get big advertisers. They wanted to feel like you thought they were special. I listened to some of them blather on for hours. In the end, I got the accounts, every time.

Chapter Thirty-Eight

PINEY FALLS, OREGON

"I was just about to tell Brother Cosmo that story when you joined us. It is such a blessing to share my experience with both of you. When the gods notified me that my plans to grow a new community - an evolved community - weren't going to work, they let me know the best way to proceed was to eliminate any pieces of my old life."

"You should have just killed yourself then. Didn't the gods speak loud enough?"

"Cosmo! Let him talk."

Zion makes the "stop" gesture with his massive hand. "No, he's right. That was one avenue. Then I realized I could still accomplish things a different way. I waited in the bushes for the right person. I had some very disobedient followers. I knew that as my commune was disbanding, the flock wouldn't go out in the world and spread my message. They had to be eliminated. Brother Randall was the first to pass. I didn't realize I had so much passion for the project until he was unrecognizable."

The room is silent as Cosmo and I contemplate that scene. Poor Cos.

"But I drug you - him - up to the falls. Your medallion was on him."

"I placed it there. Thank you for helping with my project. It was much harder to identify the body once it had been pulled up this rugged pathway. When his body made its way down stream, I removed the medal. I beat him a little longer to ensure there wasn't any bit of recognizable flesh."

"But there was. He had a scar from that horrible branding you did. It's in the autopsy report."

Cosmo stares at me. "You looked at that? Why?"

"I had a hunch." I turn to Zion. "Let's see if this other hunch is right, too. I think the former cult members who come up to the top of Piney Falls to confess their sins, or breathe in the fresh air or just enjoy the day have been accosted by you and pushed over the falls. Am I right, Zion?"

He shakes his head. "You're simplifying things. I watch all of my children. I want to make sure they are proceeding as I taught them. They come up here and confess things expressly forbidden by Fallen Branch. Do you know that Brother Nochturn was aware of my new existence and promised to continue my teachings? Twisted soul that he was, he refused to release his gambling habit. He was stealing funds from the city. He went through the city records at the end of the day and changed the things he didn't like. He insisted he knew better than I."

I think about the autopsy report attached to the death certificate. Someone wanted it found. Maybe it was Nochturn?

"What happened when he came up here? You listened in on his confession and when it didn't go like you wanted, you pushed him over the falls?"

Zion sits down beside me. I can feel some sort of electricity from his presence. The thing successful people have in common, good or bad, is a commanding presence in a room.

"What did you say your name was, Sister? I can tell you're ready to learn the ways of the universe. There are many lessons to be taught. Out here, in the woods, nature can teach them without human interference."

"Her name is none of your business, Zion." Cosmo snaps. Even though I know it's not relevant now, I gasp at Cosmo's ability to use Zion's name. In the short time I've been here, I've grown accustomed to his former followers telling me they were never allowed to use his name in his presence. Cosmo is brave today. "I believe the lady asked you a question. Why did you kill all of those people?"

"Everyone has a pre-ordained time of existence. I was privileged to know the time of each of my flock's passing."

"My father? You killed him because you were selfish. That was a fit of passion. And the mayor..." Cosmo stands and begins pacing. Knowing I'm in the room with a murderer and the man wrongly convicted of that crime is making me nervous.

"Your true father was Zion," his broad, creepy smile encompassing the entire space.

"You're nothing. Nobody. Not a parent, not an anything."

"Cos," I protest. I start imagining how many "suicides" over the years have happened. How many lives he's taken without anyone blinking an eye? I look around the room for any obvious weapons. He has to have something to kill what he eats. I see lots of nets, some crude-looking traps and baskets. No weapon.

"You must've had some help. You can't totally survive on your own," I insist.

"Sister, your intelligence shines through. There are always connections, no matter where you live. In the cities there are networks of religion, activity and culture. Out in the forest, there are networks as well. Some of us sell mushrooms to barter fo—"

I hear a loud *clunk* and Zion slumps forward. Cosmo has a large shovel in his hand. Muenster barks furiously. I look up at him in shock. "Why did you do that?"

"I was sick of listening to him blather. All those years of lectures, they just never ended. Saw the shovel behind the door when I walked in and decided I'd shut him up when I'd heard enough. We've got to get him back to town. I'm not taking any chances with this miserable lump of a human."

"How do you propose we do that?" I ask, still in

shock that I witnessed an assault...and that I feel kind of good about it.

"You've seen those old nature magazines where they strap a person between two poles and carry them? I see fishing net and poles back there. I'm going to wrap him up and we'll carry him together. At least part way down the hill. I'll call my buddy who owns Muenster and he'll meet us and call the police. You won't have to carry him very far."

"But I can't do that," I whimper. "I can barely get myself down this mountain. Its steep and—"

"There's no other way to get him out of here. By the time the police get out here, he could be long gone again. It's the only way my name will ever be cleared." He looks at me pleadingly.

"I just don't know if I..."

"I believe in you, Lanie." Cosmo smiles. I melt. It doesn't matter whether or not Dancinee is right about me manipulating him for my own needs. He has a power, too. One that leaves me weak. This crazy day has taught me that at least.

While Cosmo is fashioning a hammock, I look around the cabin. How does someone survive all of this time by themselves? There is a wooden box beside the bed. It has a large smiley face carved in the top and an additional carving that resembles the medallion. I open it tenuously and find a bundle of letters. They are in envelopes with the return address of "Fiona Sched-dy." I take the bundle and put it in my backpack.

Underneath the bed is a large collection of random

things. At first, I think he is a hoarder, but in this small space that seems almost impossible. I take pictures of each object with my phone. There are several pocket knives and a small dagger with a very ornate, pearl handle. I also find an article from a Portland newspaper: *Multiple Murderer, Nicknamed The Huckleberry Strangler, Dies in Prison Yard Scuffle.* It's dated June 10th, 1944. I tuck all of that into my back pack.

I help Cosmo bind Zion tightly and we make a deep hammock for him out of the fishing nets and a heavy tarp we found in the closet before strapping it to a long, wooden pole sitting the corner of the room. Cosmo says they are used for checking the depth of the water when he goes out to retrieve his fishing nets. Zion begins to stir.

Cosmo finds a cloth used for cleaning his dishes and stuffs it in Zion's mouth. "I can't listen to that for an hour," he remarks.

We carefully hoist the pole to our shoulders and begin walking, slowly. There are grunts and groans from inside the hammock as we move along. What a story this would make. The city girl carrying a murderer down the side of a mountain. I suppress a giggle.

By the time we reach the clearing, sweat is pouring down my face. "Wait!" I beg. "I need a minute." I can tell Cosmo is irritated. He waits for me to set my end of the pole down and then drops his end with a thud.

"We don't have much daylight left. We'll have to keep moving until my buddy meets us."

"I know. I'm doing my best." I would give anything for a latte and one of his scones right now.

"You're an amazing woman, Lanie. Hard to believe the lady who was afraid of nature a few weeks ago is able to hoist a man over her shoulder and carry him down a mountain!"

His words boost my ego and energy enough to continue. We hoist Zion to our shoulders again and he begins to squirm. Cosmo tied the hammock firm so that it wouldn't sway while we walked but he's still throwing me off balance and soon we'll be on the steep portion of the pathway.

"Listen old man, I may not have entered prison as a murderer but I know ten easy ways to make that happen now. Keep moving and you'll be the first to see if they work."

Zion becomes blessedly still.

"Lanie, I want to thank you for believing in me," He calls from over his shoulder." Other women just looked at me like a felon. I've never thought I was worthy of a relationship with anyone. At least I didn't think so until now."

"I'm lucky to know you, Cosmo Hill."

We walk the rest of the way in silence.

"'Lo?"

"Up here!" I call frantically. Hearing his voice allows my muscles to contract painfully. This body, as in tune with nature as it's become, can't take much more.

When I transfer my end to Cosmo's friend, my

shoulders begin to scream in pain. I try to keep myself upright as we walk, but I know I'm slumping forward. Cosmo and his friend are chatting happily about their capture. Finally, we make it back to my rental house. I see Vem waiting in the driveway. She comes running toward us, more interested in our capture than her beef with Cosmo.

"What kind of kill have you made? Lanie, is this the true you? Huntress? I can help you truss whatever this is." The two men set the bundle down on the driveway.

"It's no deer. It's Zion," Cosmo says in a monotone voice I've not heard him use before. He walks past her, not bothering to look her in the eyes. "Probably makes you a little sad. Also makes you a liar, November Bean."

She puts her hands up to her mouth. "This can't be. He's been here all along?"

I want to tell her about her brother, but I don't know if that will ease her pain or make it worse. I decide to wait. She walks up to the massive loaf, uncovering his face, and sniffs him. "It's him," she declares quietly. Then, for the third or fourth surprise of the day (I've lost track) she draws her leg back and kicks him hard. He winces. "That was for me." She kicks him again. "That's for Nochturn." She draws back one more time. I'm too tired to stop her.

"Don't give the cops a reason to question our capture," Cosmo's friend warns. "He'll have plenty of time to suffer in the county jail."

The police pull up as I'm making my way to the steps. My legs give out after the third step and I collapse on the cement to rest my aching body. Vem comes over and sits beside me. She rubs my back. "Lanie, you look like you've released some demons."

I look at her with surprise. "Do I? Because I think my muscles have acquired new ones. I'll be in pain for the rest of the month."

I realize I've forgotten all about the pain of losing all of my possessions and my control. I HAVE released something. The old me.

"This has been the craziest day. You were right, your visions or whatever. I did need to come to terms with some things. I'd like to tell you all about it, but I have a date with a hot bath and a bottle of wine. That is, if the locks haven't been changed." I'm filled with a sense of dread, remembering my current precarious living situation. All of my things are in the car at least.

"Why would the locks be changed?"

"Because I emailed my landlord about staying longer. Whoever this mystery person is never emailed back. I'm afraid my time is up."

"Yes, I did!" Vem stands up and puts her hands on her hips. "Why would you think I ignored you?"

"You're tooperky11? Why didn't you tell me that from the beginning?"

"Because I didn't want things to be weird with us." She paces around in a circle. "I acquired a lot of money in my divorce. I thought long and hard about what I wanted to do with it, how I could feel good about myself and still make him angry. The best idea I had was to buy homes here in Piney Falls. Fix them up and rent them out to tourists. He just hated Piney Falls." She stops and smiles broadly. "I own five homes in the area."

I dissolve in laughter. Vem joins in.

That night, I make a phone call that is long overdue.

"Dancinee? You don't have to say anything. Just let me talk for a minute. From the first day in class, you were kind to me. I'm your mother's age and you could've blown me off, but you were the only student who showed up at the hotel. When you heard about the fire, you said, 'If you need a place to crash, you can stay on my couch.' I know you didn't think I'd take you seriously. Unfortunately, no one else in my life made that gesture. I gave everyone your contact information instead of mine when I couldn't move. Even though you complained, you took care of things. I was at the lowest point in my life and you offered your hand. I just want to say thank you."

Chapter Thirty-Nine

AISLEY LUMBER TOWNSHIP, OREGON

Dearest Da,

You will find this harsh. You have such a loving heart; you don't see the bad in people. Well, you found Albert Todd to be suspect. Remember how you told him you ought not trust anyone with thick eyebrows? He did his best to convince you otherwise. Sister Faye and I laughed and laughed as we laid in bed that night. Now, looking back, we realize eyebrows or not, you were perceptive that day.

It turns out Charles wasn't the man you would've chose for me, had you known of his deceit. Albert Todd definitely would not have been the man for Sister Faye. But they gave us beautiful bairn, and without them, we would never have found ourselves in this bold, exciting land, living such a life of adventure. We had good times with them. So many good times. No

265

one could spin a yarn like my Charles. That's the way I want to think of him on my last day.

I doubt Sister Faye thinks about Albert Todd anymore. It brings her too much pain. Wouldn't it be nice to take our minds somewhere else, as she does? Maybe we are the ones who are crazy, not those like Sister Faye and Mam.

We covered our furniture and removed all of value; packed and shipped the trunks to the Widow Tweaks in Portland. It was final.

Sister Faye took Lachlan Douglas's gun from the shelf and polished it. I started to ask, "Why are you bothering with that nonsense?" Then I remembered there wasn't anything left of her mind and decided not to make a fuss. I waited patiently until she was done.

She put the bullets in it and added extra in her pocket. We walked, silently, hand-in-hand to the mill. We'd done it so many times, Da. In the early days, we would talk about what it was like to be married. Compare the brothers' thoughts and actions. They were very similar, though Charles was more focused. Albert Todd changed his mind fourteen times in the course of a day, sending poor delicate Faye in so many directions she eventually just stood still, watching it all whir by.

It was just after sunset when we reached Scheddy Cannery. There were still blues and oranges painting the horizon. "Wait," I begged. "Let's enjoy for one last time." She nodded and we paused together, listening to the sounds of the waves rolling in under the pier.

Facing our front, a world of its own, peaceful and without worry. Behind us was the noise of a town that never slept. Women calling out to passersby, selling themselves to pay for their room and board. Men, drunk and unruly, in the streets.

Mrs. Aisley tried her best to rid the town of such debauchery but was never successful. They worked against each other, Mr. and Mrs. Aisley. She wanting refinement and polite society: he, cultivating the seedy parts of life for his own financial gain. In the end they were on the same side though. She lived off the riches from his way of making money. She relished his ability to profit off the poor and unsuspecting more than her sense of right and wrong.

We were pulled back to the present grim situation by the sounds of workers yelling from within the cannery. It was common for them to have to yell over the sound of the machinery. I realized I had not only grown used to the harshness of those sounds, but looked forward to them.

Faye squeezed my hand and I knew it was time. We walked into the building one last time, into our tiny office. Mr. Samuel Li told us Mr. Stanford Aisley spent most evenings here as if he owned the place. Our office was now where he conducted his illegal activities, lest he sully his own with his misdeeds.

Normally, entering the building our noses were assaulted with the strang smell of dead fish. When both Faye and I were first carrying our bairns, we couldn't stand the smell and would have to step outside often. Mr. Samuel Li would bring fresh water and wait while our stomachs settled.

Sometimes we felt the quease all day. Once the scent infiltrated our clothes there was no way to escape it until wash day. Now, so many years later, my nostrils flared trying to find the familiar scent that went with the building. Instead, there was something similar to all of the boys' feet after a day of hard work in the garden or field. It was an assault of the senses and mind alike that caused my stomach more upset than the many years of fish smells.

Mr. Stanford Aisley was smoking a cigar, something the boys had expressly forbidden within the building because of the chance for fire. We knew he liked his cigars. There was a woman we recognized from Pragule Saloon sitting beside him, buttoning up her dress. Faye brought those women fresh baked scones for a time, thinking they were just in need of home-cooked meals to change their ways.

He looked up when we entered the room, surprised to see us. "Missus Scheddy. What a delight! Have you come to help us label cans tonight? We scheduled you for next Thursday." He twitched his thin mustache, just like the mouse I'd always pictured him to be.

"We need to speak to you. Alone." I forced the shaking from my voice. I was doing this for my family.

I glanced out the window, down at the small crew who would normally be ending the life of a sea creature. Chopping a seemingly harmless vegetable seemed more sinister. They didn't betray any signs of embarrassment on their faces. It was just another job to them.

"Of course." He turned to the safe. The safe we used to store our record books over the years. I used to think they were sacred evidence of our success. Now I knew them to be a farce. He withdrew three, crisp twenty-dollar bills and handed them to his friend.

Faye squeezed her arm as she was about to leave. "Wait. Ye have my cash in there," she said in her defiant Scottish brogue.

The woman began to protest and Mr. Stanford Aisley sighed loudly before removing a roll of money from his pocket and handing her three more bills. She shook her head but said nothing. At least this week she would eat well.

"What are you women doing here? I'd rather you weren't here while I'm working. It confuses the workers."

"We need to speak with you about selling our business to you." I sat down in my favorite chair; the one Charles crafted out of the first tree felled on our property.

Mr. Stanford Aisley twitched his mustache and leaned forward. I could smell the Norwegian liquor on his breath. "I've already tried to explain to you women that I can't possibly buy your business. We made a deal and that is to be honored by you both. And when you're gone, your sons will help me. Maybe even your daughter may be of use, Fiona." He smiled, showing his pointed, yellow teeth.

I knew we had made the right decision.

Your Devoted Dochter,

Fiona Flanagan

Dearest Da,

I felt a peace that had alluded me in these weeks of planning. "No, Mr. Aisley. Our children won't suffer at your hands." *Do it now, Faye.*

"Oh?" he chuckled. "Do you have some grand plan to change the ways of the world? I guarantee you, no woman has that kind of power. At least not in these woods."

I closed my eyes. Though I'd seen many fish gutted throughout the years, never had a rat of this size seen its ending in our establishment. There was only silence.

"Is there something else? I'm a busy man."

"Our sgian-dubh. I know you've been keeping it in your drawer." Faye was standing behind him. All she had to do is pull the trigger and we could get the knife ourselves.

"Very well." He pulled the knife from the drawer and held it tight. "But I'll expect something in return."

I reached over to grab the sgian-dubh from him. He jerked his hand away sharply from me, the point of the knife now aimed at his chest. Sister Faye shot him once and he fell forward onto its sharp blade. He grunted as she jammed the butt of the gun into his tiny head. One time, then another, then a third. Mr. Stanford Aisley clutched his chest as his blood spilled over the desk Albert Todd painstakingly sanded for days before hiring Mr. Samuel Li to smooth it to perfection. He fell to the floor and Faye pulled the knife from his chest, jabbing it into his throat.

"Nothing in return, sir," Faye said simply. I marveled at her steely countenance. She always cried when we had to put a farm animal down before its time. But never the mice. She was happy to see them devoured by the barn cats. Maybe that part of her childhood was the best preparation for our adult lives.

Faye quickly poured kerosene on the desk and struck a match. We could hear the last few gasps of air leaving Mr. Stanford Aisley's body. Faye was going to stab him again, but I insisted she leave him. "Give him a minute more to suffer in this world." I told her. I never thought I was a vindictive woman. I was wrong.

I pulled the string which blew the whistle for the building. If there weren't fisherman coming in with a new catch, it always meant there was an emergency and the workers were to leave immediately. They looked up at the office helplessly. Most of the men we normally employed worked in the lumber mill during the off season. There were some who hadn't been in the cannery before and looked at us with concern.

"Fire!" I called out, as loud as I could over the machinery. "Run! Now!"

I looked at the safe, thinking I might take all the cash and give it to the men working. I didn't recognize what was real and what wasn't. I didn't want these men to get into trouble in case there were questions later. I knew there would be a few who spent it all gambling. I didn't know which of them knew what they were actually canning. They didn't have a choice though. If they wanted to work in this town, they had to get along with Mr. Stanford Aisley.

Faye pulled on my arm. I looked at her face. She displayed the blank stare I had come to find familiar. After ending Mr. Stanford Aisley, her brain must've shut down again. I never understood how that worked.

I looked around the room one more time as it filled with smoke before leaving the building, the men gesturing excitedly. One ran off to ring the bell at the volunteer fire department, calling all who were available. Just last year Sister Faye and I purchased a new fire engine. It was a fine-looking vehicle. I'm sure there are even more wonders to come. I'm sorry I won't be able to see them.

At this point I paused. Maybe we deserved to have our ending beside Mr. Stanford Aisley. We were deceivers just like him. We gave our cannery over to can dangerous mushrooms to be sold overseas. We could have said no and walked away. We were just as greedy as he, wanting our name to stand for something. Maybe we were more deceitful. The doctors in the hospital and the patients had no idea the latest in surgical instruments were only available because of our ill-gotten gain. The children and teachers at City School opened their crisp, new books and excitedly studied the latest subjects without knowledge of how they were able to be acquired.

I felt a push on my back. "You go now!" It was Mr. Samuel Li. He forced us out of the building. Once we were outside, he gestured excitedly. "No more time for ladies. You leave now!"

Faye smiled and kissed his forehead. She handed him the bloody knife. "Take care of this family heirloom, would you dear Mr. Li?" she said sweetly.

I handed him a large parcel. "All loose ends taken care of. I'll carry my own pack now."

He nodded. I think there may have been a tear in his eye.

Sister Faye and I walked slowly up the hill. "Are you sad, Faye?" I asked. She smiled. Of course, she wasn't. This was what she wanted ever since Hiram died, then after the loss of Albert Todd. Each one chipped away another piece of her until it didn't seem worth breathing anymore. She hated the world for what it had done to her family. It was only living with my happy bairn that forced her onward all of those years.

We paused to view the Little Cone. Such a lovely

sight. This time of year, it gushed extra heavy because of the rains. I was glad it wasn't raining today. My last day. We continued on to Piney Falls, up to the rock where we seemed to solve all of life's problems.

I sat down with the pencil and paper I brought, so I could write to you, and to leave a note for Mrs. Violet Aisley. You deserve to know our true hearts, Da. We tried to be the women you and Mam wanted us to be. I wish you could've come with us to this wondrous land. Things might have been so different. You would've seen right through our husbands. Though there wouldn't be much to be done. Divorced women don't fare well, and you wouldn't want your dochters to be scorned women.

We tried to honor Mam's wishes and fulfil her dreams. I hope she is watching us; happy we came to her homeland and made a life. I can see her green eyes now, shining with memories of her life in New York.

We all try to do our best in the Flanagan family. Things don't always turn out the way we planned, but we all try. Just as you didn't mean for anything to happen to Mam, I'm sure of it. Just defending yourself and all of your bairn. See? We all have those secrets. You loved her so and I'm certain she loved you. She had that vacant look in her eyes, just like Sister Faye. We couldn't have known what would happen that day. She was always so happy and alive until then.

There was Sister Faye, milking the cows, singing her little song. Mam picked up the axe and came at her without warning. It surprised us all. It was right not to send her off. To think of her locked away, unable to enjoy the air and green hills would be too much for her as well as all of us to bear.

It was her time to go and for some reason, it had to be you that did the going. Your soul must've crumbled that day. Just like we used to put dogs down when they'd get that wild look in their eyes. You had to do it. I took all the bairn to the house while you were dealing with Mam's body, but Faye ran back. She wanted to see. She was always like that, putting herself where she shouldn't be.

Sister Faye and I did fine raising the brothers. They must be successful men now. We went on with our lives like Mam passed from a fever.

And now this is our time for goodbye. Sister Faye and I will take hand in hand and jump over these falls. It will be quick, and for that I'm thankful. That's a good way to end things, right? Sister Faye's suffering will be over. Our children are safe.

Someone will find this letter in the pocket of my coat and all will be told. Maybe they'll be happy to know all the evil in this community will be gone in one evening.

Goodbye Da.
Your Loving Dochter,
Fiona Flanagan

Chapter Forty-One

My Dearest Violet,

You took care of Sister Faye and me from the first moments we entered town. We were but shy lasses, unsure of our place in the world. Now, so many years later, we know all too well what becomes of women who haven't the smarts to take care of themselves.

Our home has been sold and the money is in an account at the bank. Mr. Samuel Li has been instructed to come in each week to receive a stipend from this account which will, in part, cover his wages as your foreman at the lumber mill.

If Mr. Samuel Li does not appear, the bank is instructed to send a letter to the US Marshals. You will be interested to learn this letter contains all the misdeeds committed by you and your husband, Mr. Stanford Aisley. The canning and shipping of drugs, kidnapping men and selling them into servitude, and the murder of Mr. Lachlan Douglas.

This is the best thing for you, dearie.

Your devoted friend,

Fiona Flanagan

Chapter Forty-Two

PINEY FALLS, OREGON

isley Lumber Township Herald
November 26th, 1925
As if our small community has not suffered enough, prominent businessman Stanford Aisley, owner of Aisley Lumber Mill, has been found to have perished in the Scheddy Cannery fire. Investigators discovered the body while searching the blackened timbers for signs of misdeeds. It was burned beyond recognition, but a pocket watch given to him by his father was observed near the body.

When notified, delicate Violet Aisley said she thought her husband to be out of town on business. A woman of steely confidence, she pushed her sorrow aside and immediately began plans to keep the mill running under her advisement.

Mr. Samuel Li, a long-time Scheddy Salmon Cannery and Aisley Lumber Mill employee, has been appointed manager by Mr. Aisley's widow, Violet. It is unclear if she plans to hire someone else to take his place.

It's three days before I can bring myself to read through all the letters Fiona Flanagan wrote to her father. They are heartbreaking and fascinating at the same time. When I get to the last one, she wrote, I find another stuck to the back. It is different handwriting, and the paper appears to be much newer.

It takes some sleuthing to get to the truth, but when I find it, there is an urgency to tell the three people who are the center of my strange little world. I quickly make some arrangements before I pull on my shoes and put my hair in a ponytail. I don't even bother to glance in the mirror.

I ring Vem's doorbell four times, enjoying the Fruity Boats song. No one answers, so I decide it's ok to let myself in. That's what she did the night we found Zion. I was in the bath, with wine. She came in with more. We sat and talked until my skin was so wrinkled, I didn't think it would ever return to its normal shape. I don't imagine she remembers some parts of her soul that she bared at the end of the second bottle.

Her house is some kind of showpiece - a 1960s showpiece, that is. The bright tangerine-orange, and even brighter red and aqua accents, are so sharp they hurt my eyes. Avocado-colored bean bag chairs dot the room. There are movie posters everywhere, from every decade. I see Tulip Sloan posed on a giant flower cushion, the promotion for the movie, *Flowers in the Wild.* For the first time, I look into her eyes. She looks sad and lonely. Not the impossible standard of perfection I spent my life trying to achieve. Just a regular woman with a hard life.

"Vem?" I call out. Nothing.

I walk timidly through the sunken living room and into the kitchen, a pristine space with mustard-colored appliances. If I go too much further, it will seem like I've come to stalk her. I start to go back when I see framed photos on the china hutch. There is one of Vem, Cedar, an unidentified boy and Cosmo, all standing arm in arm. They appear to be in their mid-teens. All are wearing the same, mud-colored shirt and medallions around their necks.

"You could have sung my name. It's been proven people respond best to the sound of music, especially when it's the human voice." I jump, feeling like a criminal. She is in crimson red today, making her appearance dramatic. Dark red lips match her headband and glasses.

"Sorry to intrude! When you didn't answer, I thought you might be in meditation in the back yard. Your house is amazing! Where did you find all of this stuff?"

"When my marriage ended, I realized I'd never given myself a chance to experience life in the real world. I decided to watch every television show, every movie, find everything relevant to modern society that would make me feel like everyone else."

I smile. "You're so much better than an 'everyone else.' Someday we'll have to talk about movies."

"Did you see my Tulip Sloan poster? Did you know that poor woman died of a drug overdose? She worked herself to death to avoid the sadness in her own life. No matter how much you resemble her, you're a much finer example of a beautiful face, Lanie."

"Thanks, Vem. She and I each worked hard so we didn't have to think about our problems. My mother once told me I'd never be as good as Tulip, no matter how many Saturdays I spent dressed up to look like her. I tried for many years to become my own version of Tulip, thinking somehow my mother would be proud. I don't think I need to be her anymore. I'm something better."

"Lanie! You've had such a breakthrough! We're not so different, really. It's my meditation and spinach brownies. The combination of the two bring clarity and..."

"Would you mind coming with me to meet up with Cosmo and Cedar?" I forgot momentarily why I came.

I consider the way I phrased that. Like a follower, not a leader. "Actually, I don't have time for you to disagree. You're coming with me. Whatever ritual that is taking place in your backyard will have to wait. You and Cosmo need to work this thing out, once and for all." I pull on her arm and surprisingly she says nothing. Her body moves willingly. I don't even stop to see if she has shoes on. She wouldn't care either way.

I slow down as we're walking to my car, aware I may be scaring her. "Is your delightful Fruity Boats doorbell also a part of your missed childhood? I can't imagine you were allowed to eat them at Fallen Branch."

"Yep. I researched everything other kids were doing. What they were eating, what they were wearing, whatever it was that made them normal. I wanted to experience that too." She lets out a loud howl and I join in. It doesn't seem weird anymore.

The rain is starting to fall as we get in my car, and I put it in gear before she can change her mind. "Are you going to tell me what's going on?"

"No. Not until we get there."

We arrive at the history center and there is parking right in front. One of my favorite things about being in a small town.

Vem gets out of the car timidly. "Are you sure? Cosmo would rather not be in the same room with me, and—"

"It's fine. It's just a few minutes." I hold her hand as we walk into the building. Cosmo and Cedar are seated in folding chairs placed in the middle of the room with an empty chair beside Cosmo. Cedar is doodling squares and Cosmo leaned back seductively in his chair. He still gives me chills, every time I see him. Dammit.

Cosmo jumps up when he sees I'm not alone. "You brought her?"

Cedar rushes over and hugs her friend. They both begin to cry, November heaving as she lets out a mournful honk. "I'm sorry. We should have fixed this long before now. Cos, I'm sorry I didn't come to you."

Cosmo glares at me. I scoot two more chairs together and motion for them all to sit.

"Now that Zion is enjoying the fine accommodations at Piney Falls City Jail, we've got issues to work out before his trial begins and turns you all topsy-turvy. There are two very important things to do. First, November, you need to tell Cosmo what you told me about the day after Zion disappeared."

She looks at me with uncertainty.

"Go ahead," I command. "No more secrets."

November stands up and begins pacing, arms clasped behind her back. "After Zion disappeared, we were all like ants exposed to daylight for the first time. Running in circles. My parents had been trying to leave for a while. They were relieved when they heard about him and just wanted to get out." She stops pacing, right in front of Cosmo. I'm worried he'll get up and punch her, but instead he looks away.

"We weren't sure if someone else would be taking over. There were several people trying to take control before everyone was gone." She closes her eyes for a moment before continuing. "That's when I was taken aside. 'Go down to the police station and say that you watched Cosmo kill Zion. If you do that, you and your family can leave peacefully. Together.' You know how much we all wanted that." She glances sideways at him. He doesn't respond.

"Some commune members wanted to make an example of you, Cosmo, so the town wouldn't think we were all killers." She begins pacing again. I hope she doesn't break into a howl or Cosmo will get up and leave and this will all be for nothing.

"I'll be honest. It wasn't a random person who came up with this bright idea. It was Nochturn. A dumb kid thinking he had a great plan to save Fallen Branch. He wanted our family to be together as much as I did. He convinced me to make the confession, so I did. By the time I returned from the police station, everyone had pretty much scattered, including my parents. All of that was for nothing."

"That's probably why Nochturn spent his life consumed with guilt," I add. "He left me several clues in the public records about Zion's true identity. He felt bad about what he did to you, Cos." I hope that's true.

"You weren't even there that night!" Cedar stands up and pushes Vem's shoulder. "I remember now, you never left the camp. How was it I didn't realize that before?"

"You were in shock. We all were. I'm...sorry."

"It doesn't help me to hang on this." Cosmo looks at his sister as he speaks. "I would have done anything to experience parents too."

"Can I feel your embrace then?" Vem opens her arms as if she expects Cosmo to fall into them.

"No. I will work on forgiving you. But I don't have to like you."

I motion for Vem to sit back down. "You all remember why I came here, right?"

"Not really," Cedar folds her arms across her chocolate brown sweater.

Vem raises her hand. "To write a book on the vast wilderness."

I shake my head. "I understand now why no one wanted to talk about the name change from Flanagan to Piney Falls."

Cedar taps her foot uncomfortably.

"Zion was given all the letters from Fiona Flanagan Scheddy. It was an inheritance from his grandfather, but we'll get to that. Fiona used them like a diary to her father. The Flanagan sisters wanted so badly to become proper business women. They did everything they could to make that happen. Opening the hospital, making the school a place for everyone, giving their employees a decent wage..."

"We realize all of this," Cosmo looks irritated, a reaction that makes me anxious. I prefer when his eyes view me adoringly.

I put my hand up. "Just wait, I promise we'll get there." Even in this very inappropriate minute, I am thinking about holding him in my arms.

"Fiona Flanagan was Zion's great-aunt. Just like her, Zion was a prolific letter writer. He wrote one to his great-grandmother Faye Flanagan. In it he explained his duty to murder everyone he encountered from Fallen Branch. Those who came up to the falls to unburden themselves - the 'weak' ones - were failures to him. To Zion, it was a violation of all the tenets of his group. If they didn't go over willingly, he stabbed them with his family's heirloom, a pearl-handled skeen-ah-DOO. That's a fancy term for a Scottish knife. That fact was confirmed on Nochturn's death certificate. I'm sorry, Vem."

"Oh, damwell golly." She sinks down in her chair and sobs for a minute. We all wait patiently for her to finish. "I wish I knew him better. I hate that he died that way."

"I know, Vem," I say softly. "If it helps, your brother wanted all of this to come out in the open. I'm sure of it. He died a hero."

"How did you find all of that information?" Cedar asks.

"Old Mrs. Petrie who works in the public records. She's got a real sweet tooth. Someone mentioned that one day while I was in the bakery. All it takes is a few muffins and a smile and she'll let you see anything."

Cosmo has leaned back in his chair, folded his arms and looks as if he might fall asleep.

"That brings me to another trip I made to see dear Gladys. When we were in Zion's cabin, I found a newspaper clipping from 1940. It was the story of a murderer, sentenced to life in the state penitentiary for murdering ten people. He hid in wooded areas, waiting for unsuspecting picnickers. When his victims wandered away from their family, he came up behind them and strangled them. He was only caught when a woman recognized him from an article about the poor Scheddy children who were orphaned after a family tragedy."

"What the Flanagan? Are you sure? One of the Flanagan kids was a murderer too? Generations of debauchery and black clouds." Vem raises her arms out wide and begins deep breathing.

"This Huckleberry Strangler, who died in prison, was Padrug Scheddy. Son of Faye, and grandfather to Zion."

"You found all of that, Lanie?" Cosmo is now fully alert.

"I also discovered all sorts of rantings Zion wrote on paper scraps. Patrick, his father, left the family early on. His mother eventually abandoned him and he grew up in foster care. At that point, Zion wanted to completely erase the Flanagan legacy. He wanted to create a perfect society because his own family was so screwed up. That's why he came here to start his cult."

"We - Cedar and I - descend from all of this madness?"

Cedar hugs her brother tightly. "If you survived Fallen Branch and then prison with your mind intact, I think you're good. We're good."

"When I got out of prison, I just wanted to put everything behind me. Instead, I should have gone to work unraveling Zion's mess. None of this is surprising, Lanie. It's impressive you put it all together though."

"But there's more. Zion was so invested in erasing his family history, he wanted to change the name of the town as well. No more town of Flanagan."

"What?" Cedar sits upright. "He wrote all of that?"

"No. When I read this, I went back and checked city records. After Zion failed in his bid to take over the town, the name was quietly changed three years later. The mayor at that time, a Mr. Chandler, was against it. He turned up at the bottom of Piney Falls."

I take a deep breath.

"In Mr. Chandler's obituary it talked about his love of Piney Falls. How he went there every weekend to think. Or, as all Fallen Branch members, to confess all of his dark secrets. That's when Zion pushed him over, but not before confiscating the medallion that you made his son, Vem."

"How would you know that, Lanie?" Cosmo asks, now genuinely engaged. "I mean, that makes a great story, but where is the proof?"

I pull out my phone and show him the picture I took in the cabin. "Do you recognize that?"

Cedar puts her hand over her mouth.

Vem gasps. "That's my Butterfly medallion. I gave that to my friend, Van, Year of the V. Our own secret identification badges. No ranking, just love. That one was courage."

"His father was Steven Chandler. He was the first mayor of Flanagan who was a former Fallen Branch member. Once he was gone, there was no one to protest the name change, the new start Zion wanted. That really began the slate of the suicides, at least that's what everyone around here assumed. It wasn't the Flanagan curse at all. It was Zion, still in control."

Vem stands and strikes a karate pose. "A woman of great intellect. To be revered. I think we should all sing your name in praise." Only Vem.

"In a moment. But thanks." I hesitate before revealing the final bit. Things are going so well. "Cedar, there's one more piece to this puzzle that only you can share."

Cedar blushes. She looks as if she might throw up right there.

Chapter Forty-Three

PINEY FALLS, OREGON

Cosmo shakes his head in disgust. "She already told us Zion was our father. What else could she know?"

I was wrong. It's not Vem he's going to deck; it's me. "These letters didn't end up in Zion's cabin by accident, did they, Cedar?"

She walks over to the large window and stares. "How did you figure that out? You have to possess some kind of magical powers, Lanie."

I let a loud guffaw slip from my mouth. Vem stares at me with admiration. "No magic. Just access to all the records I want depending on which pastry I bring." I smile at Cosmo and he looks the other direction.

"Mr. Samuel Li, the person Fiona Flanagan references in her letters, died a very rich man. In his will, he specified all the letters of Fiona Flanagan, along with the *sgian- dubh* be returned to Fiona's children. When all three children refused to receive them, they were kept in a safety deposit box at the bank, waiting for someone who cared. Decades later, someone arrived to retrieve those letters. Gladys Petrie remembers well the day Zion came to town, angry at the world and thirsty for knowledge about his Flanagan family. Those letters stayed in a box at Fallen Branch."

"But when he pretended to die, what happened to all of his things? I never thought to ask." Vem sits up straighter in her seat.

"There was only one person who had access to Zion's personal effects. One person with a key. One person who—"

"You had all of his things, Cedar? All of this time?" Cosmo rubs his chin furiously. "How much more of this deceit can I take?"

"No, brother. He gave me instructions to bury his Box of Intellect up by the falls if something were to happen to him. He showed me the spot and said it would be a new beginning, like planting a little sprout-ling. That's what I did." She begins to weep. "I couldn't imagine my life without you, and for all he had done, life without him. I just wanted the hurt to end."

Cosmo starts to cry as well, so hard his shoulders are heaving. Vem encircles them both, letting go her loudest howl. It echoes dramatically. She looks back and motions with her head for me to join.

There is power in this circle of survivors. I'm a survivor too. I can't stop the tears.

Cedar wipes her face on Cosmo's shoulder.

"You're amazing, Lanie. I had my doubts about you in the beginning, but you're just what we've needed here. We could sure use someone like you around here permanently."

I take a step back and wipe my own damp face. "I'm thinking about doing just that. It's time for a change. My brain is whirring with ideas; things we could do to make Piney Falls a real tourist destination. No more lengthy nametags."

"Ooh. I'm so glad neighbor-friend." Vem squeals. "You know the house is yours for as much time as you need."

"It may take quite a while. There's much more research to be done."

I glance at Cosmo, whose rid-rimmed are focused only on me. My heart melts.

Epilogue

"You received all the documents?" I'm trying to put on my shoes, holding my phone with just my shoulder and ear.

"Yep. Are you sure you want to do this? Seems crazy to me, but you rich people think differently from the rest of the world." Dancinee is her usual delightful self.

"It's not crazy to open a women's shelter. I trust the architects and the social workers. And most of all, I trust you. You have a good idea of what will benefit the community." I'm a little proud of myself. No, a lot proud of myself. I donated all of my land to Dancinee, who in turn wanted to open a shelter. I put together the best resources in town to make that happen. All she has to do is graduate from college and she can work there in whatever capacity she sees fit. It's all up to her.

"Well, I realize I've told you this a hundred times,

but thank you. I can't believe meeting a lady in a writing class led to all of this."

"You're welcome, Dancinee. You just needed someone who saw you. A true diamond. Oh, I just want you to know, I've been working on a serious relationship with the 'space guy.' We're taking it slow because we're both new to this. I think things will work out."

"Good job, Lanie! That has to be a challenge for you! Did you ever find all the information you needed to write your story? Which one did you decide was the most important?"

"Are you sure, Gladys? Fiona seemed like such a sensible woman."

"I'm sure, doll. According to the census, Fiona and Faye Flanagan's father died shortly after they came to America. Since the letters were never sent, Fiona may have just written those letters to unburden herself, knowing her father would never receive them."

"I've found a different story to write. About strong women and what they accomplish in life no matter how hard it gets. Maybe this isn't something to be written, but to be lived."

"I feel like you're talking about me again. Is this a veiled way of saying you're going to write my life story? That's so not cool. Not cool at all, rich lady."

"Don't worry, Dancinee, your secrets are safe with me." I hear the doorbell. "I have to go, contact me if you have any questions. I can help with the marketing aspects of your venture. Cedar and I are putting our heads together to come up with a new marketing campaign for the city of Piney Falls, but other than that, I spend my days hiking and enjoying life."

I run to the door and throw it open. "Hello, my love."

Cosmo wraps his arms around my waist and pulls me in tight. "Are you ready?"

I nod. I still haven't gotten used to seeing someone I enjoy every day. It's a process.

We walk up the trail to Piney Falls, chattering as we go. "I always thought Tulip Sloan was my nemesis - an unattainable image. No matter what I did to transform myself into this movie star, I never quite measured up. The longer I'm here, the more I realize the battle was never between the two of us. It was my mother's tortured soul at the root of the problem."

"We should sit and watch her movies. Then I'll know what the hell you're talking about," he half-smiles. "All I know of you is that you are the beautiful woman who saved me and this town. I think that's better than a dumb movie script."

Now that I can breathe on these hikes, I can take in the atmosphere. "I can almost sense Fiona's presence. Her last trip up here, the relief and sadness she was feeling. She wanted us to find those letters and tell her story. Of that I'm sure."

When we get to the top, we gaze at its beauty for a few minutes, each lost in our own thoughts.

"This is a place of endings and new beginnings," I remark. "I can't wait to see what comes next." Soon I'll sit him down and tell him everything about my past. When we've had plenty of time to digest all of the secrets of Piney Falls.

"Any day I'll get the letter from the governor, fully exonerating me."

"I know. We'll have to celebrate. Cedar and Vem too." I drink in the mist from the falls. Vem says it gives off ions of some kind, good for the soul. "Are you feeling better about Vem? She was just as confused as you and Cedar. Trying to do the right thing, but unable to figure out just what that was."

He sighs. "Yes and no. She could have gone to the police at any time and admitted she made up the whole thing. That's hard to get past. But I will. Eventually."

I nod. "I'm sorry." I put my hand over his.

"When I got out of prison, I needed help getting on my feet. The town was made up people from the cult and the townies, about half-and-half. The former cult members imagined I killed their great leader. The others didn't like anyone from the cult and just thought of me as a criminal. Makes it hard to trust anyone.

'In my mind, Vem found out I was opening a bakery and tried to stop it. All the way from California. When I was issued a business license anyway, I decided that was why she moved back. To cause trouble for me."

He turns me to face him. "I've come to recognize that worried look. Don't. We're good. I figure we've made our peace now. You're the bridge, Lanie." He looks down and reaches into his pocket. "We need good memories of this place. There's been too much pain."

I'm starting to sweat. "I agree. What do you suggest? I have some thoughts..."

He thrusts a box upward. "Proposing."

Want to read an exclusive, bonus epilogue? Click here!
Bonus Epilogue

Find out what happens next in the Piney Falls Mystery Series!
Order your copy now!
Saving Piper Moonlight
(Scroll down for a sneak peek!)